What the hell was t...

Brett was a reasonable man. He wasn't the caveman type.

Or at least, he'd never been before. Until tonight. Over Angie.

She turned and saw him, her sweet face lighting up, soft mouth lifting in that unforgettable dimpled smile. Something hot and wild rose within him. Something every bit as dangerous as his raging fury of a moment before.

It hit him. Right there on the dance floor. The hard truth came at him swift, sure and shattering as a wrecking ball.

He was wild for Angie. *Crazy* for Angie.

Married one week…and he'd gone and fallen, head over heels, for his wife.

How could this have happened?

And what in hell was he going to do about it?

Dear Reader,

I've always adored those "falling-for-the-guy-next-door" stories. You know the kind. A guy and a girl, longtime good buddies—and suddenly they're seeing each other in a whole new light.

After a disastrous relationship in the big city with the wrong kind of guy, all Angie wants is a normal, happy, settled-down life in her hometown. Brett, her lifelong friend, wants the same thing.

It *should* be so simple. They know each other so well, have so much in common. They work together, love the same movies, share the same favorite color....

The plan is so perfect: no problems, no issues, no complications. Straight from the altar to happily-ever-after.

But when the guy next door is a Bravo, it's never that simple. And love rarely goes according to plan....

Yours always,

Christine Rimmer

CHRISTINE RIMMER

MARRIED IN HASTE

Silhouette

SPECIAL EDITION®

Published by Silhouette Books

America's Publisher of Contemporary Romance

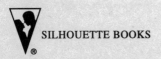

SILHOUETTE BOOKS

ISBN-13: 978-0-373-24777-6
ISBN-10:   0-373-24777-X

MARRIED IN HASTE

Visit Silhouette Books at www.eHarlequin.com

Printed in U.S.A.

Books by Christine Rimmer

CHRISTINE RIMMER

came to her profession the long way around. Before settling down to write about the magic of romance, she'd been everything from an actress to a salesclerk to a waitress. Now that she's finally found work that suits her perfectly, she insists she never had a problem keeping a job—she was merely gaining "life experience" for her future as a novelist. Christine is grateful not only for the joy she finds in writing, but for what waits when the day's work is through: a man she loves, who loves her right back, and the privilege of watching their children grow and change day to day. She lives with her family in Oklahoma. Visit Christine at her new home on the Web at www.christinerimmer.com.

For Kim and Cady,
online friends and loyal readers.
I so enjoy knowing you both.

Chapter One

Angie Dellazola gritted her teeth and bit back a groan of pain. Her sister Glory was clutching her hand so hard, the bones ground together. "Easy, Glory," Angie pleaded in a soothing tone. "Easy…"

Glory wasn't about to be soothed. Beyond mangling Angie's hand, she was screaming. And swearing: really, really bad words, words a nice Catholic girl probably shouldn't even know. Words that caused Aunt Stella, in the corner by the door to the hallway, to gasp, glance heavenward and frantically finger her rosary.

It was Angie's first day on the job at the New Bethlehem Flat Clinic—and also the day that Glory's baby had decided to be born.

Glory's water had broken forty-five minutes ago. She was fully dilated and ninety percent effaced, in active labor, swiftly approaching transition. Dr. Brett Bravo, Angie's childhood friend and now her boss, had decided that the baby was coming too fast to chance heading for the hospital fifty miles away along a tortuous mountain road. He'd opted for a home delivery in an upstairs bedroom of the Dellazola house.

"You're doing great, honey," Angie encouraged when Glory stopped screaming long enough to suck in a breath. "Try not to push quite yet. Just breathe, the way they taught you in that childbirth class—light, panting breaths and—"

"Angela Marie," Glory cut in with a guttural groan. "Don't you tell me to breathe. I *can't* breathe. It hurts too damn much…." With that, she clamped down all the harder on Angie's hand and let out another blood-curdling shriek.

Rose—Angie and Glory's mother—who hovered close on the other side of the plastic-sheeted bed, chided, "Now, Glory, honey… Angie's right. You got to go with it. Don't tense up."

Glory grunted. "I guess you didn't hear me. I said it hurts. It hurts really, really, really bad…."

"I know it hurts," said their mamma. "I've been there and you know I have." Rose wasn't exaggerating. She'd given birth to nine children—seven girls and two boys. "So I want you to listen, I want you to—"

"Listen?" Glory blew sweat-soaked hair out of her eyes. "You want me to *listen....*"

"Honey, you got to stop fighting it."

"Oh, God..." Glory shook her head wildly. "Oh, sweet Lord, here comes another one...."

From the doorway to the hall, Trista, the oldest Dellazola sister, chirped brightly, "How about some ice chips?" Trista had left her three daughters with their second sister, Clarice, and rushed over to help out. "Hel-lo?" Tris warbled again, when no one answered her the first time. "Ice chips?" Again, she got no reply—well, except for another long shriek from Glory. Trista winced. "Ice chips. Definitely. Dani will have them all ready." Danielle, downstairs in the kitchen, was the fourth sister in the family—Angie being the third. "I'll just need that bowl," Tris announced, as if anybody cared. She darted into the room long enough to grab the empty plastic bowl from the nightstand. "Be right back...." She whirled and sprinted for the stairs.

More screaming ensued. Angie submitted her hand to continued bone-grinding. Mamma Rose wiped her laboring daughter's brow with a cool cloth as Aunt Stella sent up more prayers to the virgin. Finally, the contraction peaked and faded off.

About then, Trista reappeared with the crushed ice and a spoon. She edged in between Rose and the headboard and offered the ice to Glory. Glory groaned, opened her mouth and let Trista feed it to her.

"Mmm," moaned Glory. "Good…"

"You're welcome," Trista said with a tight little smile, and offered another spoonful.

Glory started to take it—and then blinked, tossed her head to get the clammy hair out of her eyes and shot a sharp glance around the room. "Where's Dr. Brett?"

"He's here," Angie promised.

"Where? I don't see him."

"Honey. Settle down," Angie soothed. "He only went in the other room to make a couple of calls."

"I need him," moaned Glory. "I need my doctor. I need him *now*…."

"Glory. He'll be back in a minute. He's on with another patient. You're fine, honey. Relax."

"Stop calling me honey—and don't you tell me I'm fine. I'm *not* fine. I'm dyin' here."

"You are not dying," said their mother sharply. "You are doing just fine. If you were having any problems, Dr. Brett would have you airlifted to the hospital and you know that very well."

"Drugs!" shouted Glory, "I need 'em! I need 'em now!"

Right then, Old Tony, the Dellazola sisters' great-grandfather, stuck his shiny almost-bald head in the door. He swore in Italian, of which he knew very little. No one in the family did. They were several generations removed from the Old Country, after all. And Old Tony had grown up in a time when folks chose fitting in over honoring their roots. He demanded, "Can you tone it down a little in here? Man can't hear his own self think—and Dani's down in the kitchen bawlin' her eyes out. What's she cryin' about?"

Not one of the five women in the room answered him. Instead they all turned in unison and pinned the family patriarch with a look. That look was too much for any man—even Old Tony, who as a rule never let anyone, especially a woman, get the better of him.

"Humph," he said, pivoting on his heel and stumping off toward his room, shaking his head as he went.

As soon as he was out of sight, Rose sent Trista a questioning glance.

Tris rolled her eyes. "Oh, Mamma. You know how Dani gets. She wants a baby herself so bad…" Danielle and her husband, Ike, had been trying for five years to have a baby—so far without success. "It hurts her, bad, to see everyone else just popping them out when she hasn't even managed to get pregnant yet."

"Popping them out?" repeated Glory, brown eyes bugging.

"Oh, you know what I mean."

"I do—and I don't like it. And what the hell? It hurts *her?* She doesn't know what hurting is!"

Trista, unwisely, rushed to Dani's defense. "Oh, yes, she does. She's a married woman with a nice husband who only wants a little one to—"

Glory let out a shriek—of outrage that time, rather than agony. "Oh, right. Since I'm not married, I don't *deserve* this baby. Is that what you're saying, Tris?"

Trista was suddenly looking very noble. "I'm saying, there's pain. And there's pain…"

"Oh. Oh, really? Well, you know what? You can take your bowl of ice chips and you can stick it where the—"

"Shh, now," Rose cut in, patting Glory's shoulder, sending Trista a reproachful look. "Enough."

Tris shut her mouth. But Glory didn't. Another contraction took her and she started screaming again. Aunt Stella prayed and Angie soothed. Rose stroked Glory's shoulder and Trista, gravely insulted but determined to be helpful anyway, stood ready with her plastic bowl of crushed ice.

When that contraction finally eased off, a slurred male voice demanded from the doorway, "Glory. Damn you, woman." Angie glanced toward the sound.

Wouldn't you know? Bowie Bravo.

Dani, who should have stopped him at the door, was hard on his heels. Tears coursing down her cheeks, she grabbed for his arm. "Bowie. I told you, you can't come in here now."

He jerked free of her grip, his bleary gaze pinned on Glory. "Listen. Glory. Is' okay. I forgive you for all the times you said no. Jus' tell me now. Jus' say tha' you'll marry me."

Glory told him what she'd been telling him for months. "No. I won't. Now, get out."

Bowie didn't move—well, except to weave from side to side and to squint as if he were seeing two

Glories instead of just one. "Aw. C'mon. Jus' say it. Jus' gimme one li'l ol' yes."

Glory didn't say yes. She *did* make a low, growling sound. "I mean it, Bowie. I'm very busy and I can't—" she paused long enough to let out a moan "—deal with you now. So go on. Get out."

Dani swiped at her running nose, dashed fat tears from her cheeks—and grabbed Bowie's arm again. "Come on. You heard what she said."

"Hell, no." Bowie shook Dani off again—hard enough that time that she staggered and almost fell. "I ain't leavin'." He lurched into the room. "Glory. Glory, please…"

Like his three brothers—one of whom was still on the phone in the other room—Bowie was a ruggedly handsome man. Or he had been, until he'd started drinking so much. Nowadays, to appreciate his natural good looks, you had to get past the lurching walk, the slurred speech, the gray complexion and the constantly squinting bloodshot eyes. The drinking, folks in town claimed, had begun when Glory started telling him no; the more Glory told him no, the more he drank.

Bowie took another reeling step toward the bed. "Glory. Say yes…"

"Now, honey…" Rose patted Glory's shoulder. "He *is* your baby's father. Maybe if you would just—"

"Mamma. Don't you start." Sweat flew as Glory whipped her head around to glare at Angie. "Get. Him. Out. Of. Here." Glory panted each word. Then the next contraction tightened her belly. She threw back her head and let loose with more shrieking.

While Glory shrieked, the rest of the women finally got mobilized. Rose and Tris stepped to the foot of the bed and directly into Bowie's path. Angie joined them a few seconds later—once she succeeded in prying Glory's fingers loose of their death grip on her hand. Aunt Stella scooted around Bowie and fell in beside Angie. Even Dani, still sobbing softly, managed to dodge past the drunken father-to-be and take her place in the row of women.

"Outta my way," Bowie commanded, squinting harder than ever and weaving from side to side. The women held their ground.

"Come on, now, Bowie, give it up." Angie had to shout to be heard over Glory's screams.

Bowie muttered something unpleasant. He took another step toward them, sucked in a big breath and shouted, "Stan' aside, all you women. Stan' aside, now, or I won' be responsible."

"Bowie," said a deep, sure voice from the doorway.

Brett. Sweet relief poured through Angie. Her new boss had finally gotten off the damn phone. Brett would know what to do. He would handle his brother....

"Huh?" Reeling, Bowie turned. "Brett?"

"You have to go now, Bowie." Brett spoke so gently, yet even over Glory's wails of pain, every word was clear. It was one of the things Angie most admired about him. He rarely raised his voice. He might have been born a Bravo, but Brett wasn't like Bowie. Brett was levelheaded. A truly rational man.

Bowie shook his wild blond head. "I can't leave, Brett. I jus' can't…."

"You have to. For the baby's sake. For Glory's, too."

"No…" A shudder went through Bowie. In spite of all the trouble the damn idiot was making, Angie's heart ached for him.

Brett stepped forward. He took his brother by the shoulders. "You're drunk. You're only in the way here. Time to go now, and I think you know it."

There was one of those moments, the kind that always happened when two Bravos stood toe-to-toe— even if one of them was Dr. Brett, who was known to be reasonable and not prone to brawling. The row of women at the foot of the bed held their collective breaths. Glory even stopped screaming.

Bowie stiffened—causing Trista to gasp and Aunt Stella to send up a fervent, "Sweet Mother Mary…"

They all just *knew* that Bowie was going to do what Bowie always did lately—haul back his big fist and send it flying toward Brett's square jaw. One entire second passed. Two. Time drew out and hung suspended on the slender thread of Bowie's drunken indecision.

And then, from the bed, Glory let out a whimper.

The pitiful sound seemed to strike Bowie like a blow. His big body jerked like a puppet on a string— and then he crumpled forward into his brother's arms.

Brett caught him. He whispered something in Bowie's ear.

Bowie gathered himself, swaying until he achieved a shaky balance on unsteady feet. "Okay. I'm gone," he mumbled bleakly.

Brett clapped him on the shoulder, a gesture that seemed to speak of understanding and support. Without another word, head hung low, Bowie lurched around Brett and out into the hall.

No one in the room moved or made a sound—except for Glory, who held her giant belly and whimpered softly to herself. The rest of them waited, listening to Bowie's heavy footsteps moving along the upper hall, down the stairs and on through the front hall. *Clump, clump, clump.* They heard the front door open. *Clump, clump.* Bowie slammed the door behind him.

A moment of silence, then Dani sniffled. "He's gone. Thank God."

"For now, at least," Brett said with a weary shrug as Aunt Stella crossed herself. He told Dani, "Go down and lock up—the side and back doors, too. Shut and latch any windows that might be open. I don't think he'll be coming back, but there's no reason to make it easy for him if he does."

With a nod and another sniffle, Dani left the room.

Glory's whimper turned to a wail.

Brett caught Angie's eye. He grinned the grin she'd known since childhood. She grinned back, thinking how, in spite of the never-ending family drama, she *was* glad to be home again. "I'd better scrub up," he said. "I'm guessing it's about time for this girl to start pushing."

Twenty minutes later the baby's head crowned. It was not a quiet moment.

Glory alternately strained and screamed. Aunt Stella loudly prayed. Dani stared out the window and sobbed uncontrollably for the child she'd yet to conceive.

It got worse. Great-Grandpa Tony beat his fist on the wall of his bedroom and shouted, "Quiet!" and Rose yelled back, "You be quiet, yourself!" and downstairs, Bowie had returned to pound on the front door and holler, "Le' me in! S'my baby, too! I don' care wha' you say. I got a righ' to be there!"

And then, smack in the middle of all the insanity, Brett looked up from between Glory's legs and straight at Angie.

Their gazes locked and Angie felt....

Peace. A beautiful moment of glowing stillness and perfect understanding.

No doubt about it. She and Brett were the only sane people in a madhouse of screaming, pounding, shouting, begging, praying, ranting fools.

Chapter Two

That evening, Brett asked his new nurse out for a first-day-on-the-job dinner at the Nugget Steak House on Main Street. He appreciated what a trooper she'd been at Glory's delivery. Plus, sharing a drink and a meal would give the two of them a chance to do a little catching up—both professionally and as lifelong friends who'd been too long out of touch.

They took a booth. As soon as they got their drinks, Brett offered a toast.

"To Jonathan Charles Dellazola."

"Eight pounds, two ounces, with all his cute little fingers and toes." Angie raised her vodka tonic and tapped her glass to his.

Brett thought of his wild youngest brother. "Bowie's going to be furious."

Angie sighed. "Because Glory didn't give the baby his last name, you mean?" Brett saluted her again with his whiskey glass and Angie shook her head. "Oh, Brett. I know he's your brother, but…"

"Yeah. He's a mess. Lately, he's not getting much of anything right. Drinking all the time. Can't hold a job…" Brett felt the wry smile as it twisted his lips. "Not that he ever was much good at being any man's employee—and you know what?"

She nodded. "It's not our problem. Your little brother and my baby sister have to work it out between themselves."

"You always were a quick study."

"Some things, it doesn't take a genius to figure out."

Nadine Stout, headwaitress and half owner of the Nugget, sauntered up to their booth and dropped a basket of hot rolls on the table between them. "You two need more time?"

Angie spoke right up. "Not me. I'll have the New York steak, medium-rare. Green salad. Italian dressing."

Brett did like a woman who knew how to order. Angie had never been the kind to dither and stall. "I'll have the same. But make my steak rare."

Nadine scribbled on her order pad. When she had it down, she stuck her pencil behind her ear. "Angie, I said it once and I'll say it again. It's real good to have you back home."

"Glad to be back." Like her six sisters, Angie was a pretty woman. Also like her sisters, cute dimples appeared in her cheeks when she smiled.

Nadine said, "I hear you're workin' at the clinic now."

"That's right."

The waitress aimed a joking scowl in Brett's direction. "This one better treat you right."

"Well, it's only my first day, but so far, so good."

"How's Glory doing?"

"She's fine. Tired."

"I'll bet. Easy labor, I heard."

Angie sent Brett a look. He knew she was remembering all the yelling and screaming. "Well," she told Nadine. "It *was* fast."

"A little boy?"

"That's right." Angie repeated the baby's name and birth weight.

Nadine said, "You give her my best."

"You know I will."

The waitress left them.

"Word does get around, doesn't it?" Angie smoothed her napkin on her lap.

Brett sipped his whiskey. "In case you might have forgotten while you were away, in this town, there are no secrets. What you whisper to your best friend in the morning—"

"—will be shouted from the rooftops by noon," she finished for him. "I know, I know…" The light from the wagon-wheel chandelier overhead brought out red glints in her thick brown hair. Back in high school, she'd worn her hair short. It was shoulder-length now, pinned up at the moment into a soft knot at the back of her head. A few strands had gotten free and curled softly along her cheeks. She said, kind of wistfully, "The honest truth is, I've missed this town."

"Missed everybody minding everyone else's business, you mean?"

"Okay," she conceded. "Not that. But the *caring,* you know? That's the great thing about the Flat. People do care about each other, they truly do." She laughed then, and Brett thought how *he'd* missed the warm, happy sound of her laughter—though he hadn't realized it until right then. "They *care.*" Her brown eyes gleamed. "That's why they're all so damn nosy."

"Yeah." Brett loved living in the Flat. But he hated the way people gossiped. All his life, people had whispered about his family, about his bad—and mostly absent—dad, Blake Bravo. About his wild oldest brother and his crazy youngest one. "I've learned to give them nothing to gossip about."

She teased, "Oh, they talk about you, anyway. You know they do."

"You think so, huh?"

"I know so. I've heard them. They think you should settle down. Both you and Brand." At twenty-nine, a year younger than Brett, Brand was the town lawyer. Like Brett, Brand prided himself on being one of the *normal* Bravo brothers: meaning he had a decent job and he stayed out of trouble. Angie added, "In case nobody told you to your face, around here being a confirmed bachelor is frowned upon, especially if you happen to be a doctor. Or a lawyer. Ask my mamma. She'll tell you that doctors and lawyers owe it to society to marry and support a family—preferably a large one."

He faked a look of mindless terror. "You are really scaring me now."

"Oh, I'll just bet."

Brett told himself it didn't bother him that everyone thought he should hurry up and get married. "Maybe they do talk about me around town. But I promise you, it's never about how crazy, broke and out of control I am."

She looked at him steadily, her expression—what? Admiring, maybe. He liked that idea: Angie admiring him. She said softly, "You sound so proud."

He felt vaguely self-conscious and hoped it didn't show. "All I'm saying is that I make it a point to lead a very boring, ordinary, undramatic life."

"Undramatic," she repeated, and blew out a breath. "I can so relate."

Brett knew she meant because of her family. Dellazolas had lived in the Flat for a century and a half, since about 1850, when Tony and Stefano Dellazola got off the boat from Genoa at Ellis Island and decided to try their hands in the gold fields of California. They'd made the trek across the continent and they'd struck it rich working a claim a few miles up the river. The older of the two brothers, Stefano, didn't survive to have children. But Tony did.

From then on, down the generations, the first-born Dellazola male was always named Anthony. Often there would be three or four Tony Dellazolas alive at one time. They always had different nicknames: Old Tony, who was Glory's great-granddad; Little Tony, Angie's dad; Anthony, Angie's big brother and Baby Tony, Anthony's son.

The Dellazolas were a rowdy bunch. There were a lot of them and they all seemed to live by the credo that anything worth saying was worth shouting out good and loud.

Angie sipped from her drink again. "So. What have you been up to for the past...what is it? Twelve years since you headed for UC Davis?"

He pretended to look surprised. "Twelve years? Has it been that long?"

She made a soft sound in her throat. "It has."

"Well, there was the usual—college and med school and my residency."

"And now you're back in town. My mother, by the way, is thrilled that you took over when Doc Hennessey decided to retire."

"If Mamma Rose is happy, I'm happy—and in the eleven years I was away, I did manage to get back home at least five or six times a year. Unlike *some* people I could mention."

"Okay, okay. I should have come back more often

and I know it." She showed those dimples again—but her eyes, he thought, looked kind of sad. "What can I say? You know how it goes. Life happens. A girl doesn't make it home as often as she should and before you know it, a decade has gone by…." Her voice trailed off.

Brett felt no rush to fill the silence that fell between them. Funny. He'd always been comfortable with Angie. Since way back when she was eight and he was ten and she'd taken to tagging along after him wherever he went. He hadn't minded her hanging around him. He hadn't had a lot of friends as a kid. Back then, he'd been a loner and kind of shy. After school, he'd liked to take a book or a fishing pole and wander the surrounding hillsides, following the deer trails beneath the shadows of the tall trees.

Angie was self-reliant, even as a little girl. She'd made it a point of pride to keep up, no matter where he led. Most important, she hadn't found it necessary to fill every silence with breathless chatter. He studied her across the knotty-pine table of their booth.

She looked at him sideways. "What?"

"Just thinking how some things stay the same, no matter how many years go by. You remember that jail we built down by the river?"

"Out of willow branches. Oh, yeah." Her eyes were bright with the memory. "Lashed it all together with bark. That amazed me. How you made those long strips with your pocketknife and they were strong as lengths of rope. I was way impressed, I have to tell you." She made a sound midway between a grunt and a chuckle. "And then Buck came along…" Buck was the oldest of his three brothers. "He tied us together, remember?"

"How could I forget? Locked us both in our own damn jail." Brett teased, "You always had a big crush on Buck."

She didn't even blush. "Every girl in town had a big crush on Buck. He was so wild, he made Bowie look tame by comparison."

"Buck's doing great, did you know?"

"Oh, yeah. A world-famous author, no less." Buck was now a successful journalist. He'd also written a bestselling book about the Texas oil industry.

"He got married," Brett added on the off chance she hadn't heard.

But of course, she had. "To some good-lookin' rich woman from New York City."

"B.J.'s her name," he said.

"She's expecting, isn't she?"

"That's right. Her baby's due next month."

Angie stared into the middle distance, a musing look on her face. "Buck Bravo, a big success—not to mention, about to be a dad. Who would have thought it?"

Brett sipped more whiskey. "So you heard the whole story, huh?"

"Yep. Glory told me everything. She really likes Buck's wife. They keep in touch. You can bet Glory's already called New York City to tell B.J. the big news about baby John."

Nadine trotted up with their salads. "Look at you two. Just like old times, huh?" The bossy, tough-talking waitress actually had a sentimental gleam in her eye. "Brett and his sidekick…"

"Smile when you say that." Angie pretended to look dangerous.

Nadine put on her usual don't-mess-with-me scowl. "Just eat your salads." She plunked them down and strutted off.

They dug in, reminiscing as they ate. The steaks came. They talked some more.

After Nadine had cleared off their empty plates and brought them coffee, they hung around. Why not? It had been over a decade. They had a lot of catching up to do.

And then there was the work they shared. Brett brought her up to speed on the ins and outs at the clinic and outlined some of the changes he hoped to make, most of which were going to cost money way beyond their operating budget.

"Some things take time," he said. "As of now, we're doing damn well. A doctor *and* an R.N. on staff. Most small-town clinics are lucky to get one or the other."

"As long as you're grateful," Angie said jokingly. She wasn't making anything approaching what she could get elsewhere.

Neither was he, for that matter. "Hey. We both know you didn't come home to the Flat to get rich."

"That's right—and refresh my memory. Why *did* I move back home?"

"The way everybody *cares*," he said, trying to look grave. "The chance to be close, once again, to the friendly, loving, gentle people you've known all your life."

"Ah." She made a wry face. "I knew there was something." And they laughed together. Then she said, "Really, you *are* doing well. Not even two years out of your residency and my mamma says you own your own house."

"I'll let you in on my secret. Three little words. No student loans."

"Scholarships?"

"Some. But they didn't cover everything. I worked, when I could find the time—which there's never enough of in med school."

"So…?"

"I learned to write grants. You'd be surprised how many big grants go begging because no one applies for them—or if they do, they don't qualify."

Her eyes lit up. "That's right. You've gotten grants for the clinic, too, haven't you? You said the day you hired me that grant money would be paying a lot of my salary…."

"A small-town doctor has got to use every resource at his disposal just to keep things up and running."

"Smart," she said in that admiring tone that made him feel about ten feet tall. "You always were very, very smart."

An easy silence fell. After a moment he heard himself admit, "Okay. It does freak me out a little. That people talk about me."

"Brett. Come on. It's the Flat. They talk about *everybody*. You got your equal opportunity gossipers around here."

"But, damn. It's just not right. I've made one hell of an effort to be the kind of guy nobody would ever talk about."

"You mean, a reasonable guy? A levelheaded, responsible guy? The kind of guy people trust and look up to?"

"Yeah."

"Then stop worrying. That's just what you are. People respect and admire you. You're a fine doctor and they all know it—and folks around here will talk about someone they respect *almost* as often as they'll talk about the wild and crazy ones."

He felt right next door to gratified. "When you explain it that way, it sounds like a good thing."

"Hey. Probably because it *is* a good thing—even if it does mean every unmarried girl in the county is out to get your ring on her finger."

He leaned close to her again and lowered his voice. "The truth is, I am going to get married. I want that. Marriage. But not until I find the right woman—a woman who wants what *I* want out of life."

"Oh, I do understand."

He shot a glance around the restaurant. There was no one near their table. "And, well, keep it to yourself but…"

"You know I will. I won't say a word."

He believed her. Angie had always been good at

keeping her mouth shut when it mattered. "There *was* someone. Someone serious. While I was still in med school." He heard himself telling her what nobody else in the Flat knew and it seemed…right. It felt *good*. To finally tell someone he knew he could trust. "Her name was Lisa. I was crazy for her…."

Angie was shaking her head. "Crazy. That's a dangerous word, Brett."

"Yeah. Tell me about it."

"It ended…badly?"

"A real mess. She had mood swings. Serious ones."

"Bipolar?"

"The symptoms were all there. But while we were together, she would never get help. So I hesitate to diagnose her out of hand. She was deep into self-medicating. Alcohol. Prescription painkillers."

"Oh, Brett. I'm so sorry."

"I finally broke it off with her. It was…I was still wild for her when I told her it was over. It hurt like hell, to end it. I was a wreck for months, almost dropped out of school. But slowly, I got back on track. She went into treatment finally. I lost touch with her after that."

"Do you still…?"

"Love her? Uh-uh. I think back on it and all I feel is sorry for her. She was such a mess. And I was such a fool—and that's what bothers me, you know? That I would fall for one of the wild and troubled ones, when I know better. When I've always sworn that the drama queens just aren't for me."

"Oh, yeah. I understand. Completely."

"And I can tell you this much…"

She said it for him. "Never again."

"Exactly."

Nadine strolled by and refilled their coffee cups. They watched her saunter off.

When they were alone once more, Angie said, "Really, Brett. I do know. I know just what you mean." She licked her soft lips and swallowed. "It, um, happened to me, too."

"You're kidding." Not Angie, he thought. She would never fall for some wild-ass fool.

But then she said, "I'm not kidding, truly I'm not— and I shouldn't be telling you." Her cheeks had flushed pink. She cast a glance at the knotty-pine ceiling. "Way to go, Angela. First day on the job and you tell your new boss what a total imbecile you are."

"Hey."

She wrinkled her cute nose at him. "What?"

"I may be your boss, but I'm also your friend. And besides, I just told *you* what an idiot *I* was."

"Well." She suppressed a smile. "There is that."

"Tell me," he commanded.

She narrowed her eyes like the villain in some old-time Western movie. "You will never tell anyone. Ever."

"Absolutely. Never. You have my word."

"Nobody else knows. Except Glory, I did tell her. And my mother suspects—I mean, that *something* bad went on. But I don't want it all over town. I truly do not."

He put up a hand, like a witness swearing an oath.

"What happens at this table, *stays* at this table." Still, she hesitated. "Angie. Come *on*."

She grumbled, "Mine's worse than yours…."

"Impossible."

"God. You'll probably fire me when I tell you. You shouldn't have someone so stupid working for you. I'm not kidding. I was the pinnacle. The queen. The *empress* of stupid."

"I'm not going to fire you. Talk."

"Oh, God…"

"Talk."

"Six months ago, in San Francisco?"

"Yeah?"

"I fell and I fell hard for a really, really bad guy—I mean, we say how bad Buck used be. We shake our heads over Bowie. But there was never any doubt that both of them are good men, with good hearts, deep down. You know?"

"Yeah. I know."

"Oh, Brett. It was pitiful. *I* was pitiful. His name was Jody Sykes. He had muscles on his muscles and he drove this mean black Harley and when I'd hear the rumble of that big, ol' engine pulling up outside my apartment…"

Brett got the picture. "Hot and heavy, huh?"

"Oh, yeah. Hot and heavy. I would go up in flames every time he got near me. My girlfriends all warned me about him. They could see right through him. They gently reminded me how he was using me, living off me. They patiently pointed out how he'd moved into my apartment, how I paid all the bills and bought all the food, how he didn't have a job and didn't look too likely to be getting one anytime soon. A couple of my friends even claimed he'd made passes at *them*."

"And you didn't believe them?"

She pressed her lips together, shook her head. "I thought they were just jealous—because Jody was such a *prize*. I told them they were wrong. That they didn't understand him. And guess what happened?" She answered her own question. "Well, just what you might think would happen. Three months ago, I came home from pulling a double shift at the hospital to find Jody in *my* bed—with a very naked blonde."

"You kicked him the hell out on the spot, right?"

"Well, I tried. The blonde, at least, had the consideration to go. She grabbed her clothes and ran. But Jody wouldn't budge. He sat there, butt-naked in my bed, and called me all kinds of names, said he would leave when he was damn good and ready to go. Things got uglier. I swear, up till then, he'd never hit me. I may be the empress of stupid, but I do have the sense to get out fast if a man raises his hand to me. That was the day I learned that for a guy like Jody, there's always a first time. I'm not a big shouter, you know that. I was raised with shouters and I always swore I'd never be one. But I did shout that day. I yelled at that S.O.B. to get out of my apartment and out of my life. I yelled— and he hit me. He kept on hitting me."

Brett had never been one to settle an issue with his fists. Still, he found himself hoping that someday he might run into Jody Sykes, just for the pleasure of re-arranging his face for him. "Sonofa—"

"Somebody in my building called the cops. Finally they came and took him away. I went down to the police station and pressed assault charges against him. He got bail. And promptly vanished."

"Good riddance."

"No kidding. I threw all his stuff in the street. I was furious and brokenhearted and black and blue—all at the same time. Worst day of my life. Or so I thought. Until I got that notice from my bank that my checks were bouncing."

"The bastard stole your checkbook?"

"I figure he must have gotten hold of one of my deposit slips. And somehow he'd faked an ID and sent in some woman to pose as me."

"Tell me they caught him. Tell me he's doing some serious hard time."

Slowly and sadly, she shook her head. "Not so far."

"He took all the money you had?"

"I had some in savings. He didn't get that."

"Damn it, Angie." He reached across the table. She put her hand in his. He gave her slender fingers a squeeze. "That's why you came home?"

Those slim shoulders drooped. "Yeah. A lot of the reason. San Francisco's a beautiful city. But Jody kind of ruined it for me. The weeks went by. My bruises healed. I still had some savings, a cute apartment and a real good job with great benefits. But all I could think about was home, you know? About how safe it is here. About how, here in the Flat, something like what Jody did to me would never happen—or if it did, one of my brothers or you or Brand or even Bowie would beat the crap out of that dirty you-know-what before he could get out of town."

Brett said, "Beating the crap out of bad guys isn't really my style—but in this case, I might have to consider making an exception."

She made a low sound. "Whatever you did, however you handled it, I know you would have found a way to make it real clear to Jody that he'd better do right by me, or he'd be sorry."

"It's good," he said. "Good you came home."

"Yeah. I know— Oh, Brett, it was terrible." Shadows stole the light from those soft brown eyes. "He broke my heart, beat me up—and then he ran off with my money. Oh, I've learned my lesson. It's not worth it, to go nuts over some wild man, not even with the great sex thrown in. Like you said. Never again. From now on, I just want a life that's…"

He said the word for her. "Normal."

She met his eyes. "Normal. Yes. That's exactly it."

Nadine was coming their way. Brett realized he was still holding Angie's hand across the table. Feeling suddenly sheepish, he let her go.

"Okay, you two," Nadine said gruffly. "Closing

time." She gestured at the clock on the wall over the door.

Damned if wasn't eleven-thirty. Brett glanced around the dining room. The chairs were up on the tables. All the other customers were gone.

"Eleven-thirty?" Angie sounded just as surprised as he felt. "It can't be."

Nadine laughed her rough-and-ready laugh. "Well, you two had a lot of years to catch up on."

"Yeah, we did." Angie sent him a conspiratorial glance. "A lot of years…"

Brett put the money on the table, including a giant-size tip to cover all the hours they'd been sitting there. He helped Angie into her jacket and they went out into the chilly May night.

Main Street was all but deserted. Across from the Nugget, at the St. Thomas Bar, the lights were still on. Intermittent laughter came to them faintly from behind the bar's studded double doors. The Victorian-style streetlamps made soft pools of light on the empty street and overhead, the crescent moon seemed to dangle from the brightest star.

Angie stepped out from under the tin roof that jutted over the sidewalk and into the middle of the deserted street. She tipped her head back to the black, star-thick sky. "Oh, Brett. Look at all those stars. So bright. So thick. You don't see stars like that in the city." She put out both arms and she turned in a circle, looking up— at the sky, at the dark shadows of the trees that covered the mountains all around them. When she got back to where she started, facing him again, she sucked in a big breath through her nose. "Mmm. Cedar. And wood smoke. I've been missing those smells for years without really even knowing that I did." She lowered her head and looked at him, white teeth flashing, the shadow of that dimple appearing on her cheek. "Isn't it funny? How you can miss something and not even realize you do?"

"Yeah." He held out his hand to her. "It's funny how that goes."

She hurried back to him. He tucked her fingers into the curve of his elbow and walked her to the intersection of Commerce Lane. From there, they went their separate ways—Angie to the cottage on the hill behind her mother's house on Jewel Street, and Brett to his own place, down by the river on Catalpa Way.

Angie had thought her first day on the job was a busy one.

The second made the first seem like a walk in the park. It was one thing after another, all day long.

An old miner who worked a dredge on the river about four miles south of town cut half his foot off chopping wood. His partner brought him in, along with the severed section of foot. Brett patched the old guy up as best he could, put the section of foot on ice and called for the helicopter to get him to the E.R. in Grass Valley.

Then Alma Sweat up the hill behind the courthouse on Holloway Road had a heart attack. They had to call for the helicopter again.

Bowie came in, looking like the walking dead, with a gash on his jaw that needed ten stitches. He claimed he'd run into a door.

They treated two cases of pneumonia, a couple of kids with strep throat, and the whole Winkle family— Nan and George Winkle and their three kids, who were eleven, seven and five. The Winkles all arrived together, groaning and holding their stomachs. The five-year-old walked in the door and promptly vomited. The seven-year-old followed suit. Mina, the clinic receptionist, was not the least amused.

Brett examined them, one after the other and delivered his diagnosis: food poisoning. He sent the family home with instructions to drink a lot of fluids and take care to replenish their electrolytes. "And call," he cautioned, "if your symptoms aren't significantly improved within forty-eight hours."

By then, it was lunchtime. Or it would have been. If one of the Jackson kids hadn't decided to race his bike down Church Street. He ran right into sweet old Sidney Potter, who was huffing her way up the steep street on foot.

When the dust settled, the Jackson boy and Sidney each had a broken leg. Fortunately, in both cases, they were simple fractures. Brett and Angie were able to set them right there at the clinic.

And after that?

More of the same.

Every time they dared to hope they might get a break, another minor emergency came lurching in the door. At six, an hour later than usual, they closed for the day.

Mina, with kids at home, couldn't wait to get out of there. "See you tomorrow," she called as she rushed out the door.

Brett turned to Angie. "Dinner?"

She'd been hoping he might ask. "As long you let me pick up the check."

"Done."

At the Nugget, the booth they'd sat in the night before was waiting. Okay, it was kind of dumb, but already Angie thought of it as "their" booth.

They both ordered the roast chicken and cheesy potatoes and they talked. And talked.

The subject of love and marriage came up again. Angie listened, rapt, as Brett confided, "The whole love and passion and over-the-moon thing. I just don't trust it. I've got a theory about it. Don't laugh…"

"I won't. I swear."

"You know last night, when we were talking about how we both wanted things 'normal'?"

"Oh, yes. I remember."

"Well, I'm thinking that, when you want things normal, that means you can forget about falling in love—and no, I don't mean you can't love the one you marry. Love's important. But the whole '*falling* in love' thing. Uh-uh. I'd even go so far as to say that a great love—or whatever you want to call it—a wild, crazy, passionate all-consuming love?"

"Yeah?"

"It isn't normal in the least. It's a…chemical reaction, an imbalance. A dangerous one. Nature's way of making sure the species continues. When you're crazy in love, you're all out of balance. And maybe, if you want a good life, a rational life, well, you just don't get a great love. I'm thinking I'm okay with that, for myself. I've seen great loves crash and burn. Take my mother." His mother, Chastity Bravo, owned and ran the Sierra Star, a bed-and-breakfast across the Deely Bridge on Commerce Lane. "My mother loved my psycho father with a passion and a dedication that lasted decades." The story was something of a legend in the Flat, how Chastity had remained true to Blake Bravo, though he was hardly ever around. "He'd been out of her life for almost twenty years when she learned that he was a murderer and a kidnapper. That he'd 'married' a lot of other women all over the country and had kids with them, just like he did with her. She almost died when she found out, did you know that?"

Angie shook head. "Poor Chastity…"

"She almost died," he said it again, as if he still couldn't believe it. "And not because he'd betrayed her and lied to her and walked out on her and never come back. Uh-uh. She almost died of *grief* because, when she learned all those awful things about him, she also learned that he'd died in an Oklahoma hospital a few months before. *That's* what nearly finished her off, finally knowing for certain he was really gone, that there was no chance she'd ever see him again."

"Unbelievable," said Angie.

"Yeah. Pitiful. *That's* crazy love." He drank from his water glass. "And then there's the way that Bowie loves Glory. I mean, I do believe that he loves her. Wildly. To distraction and back again. But look at him. What good is a love like that? It's killing him."

"I see your point. I really do."

"So this is how I look at it. It's a trade-off. A wild, crazy, once-in-a-lifetime love. Or a sane life. I'm taking sanity. Hands down."

"Oh, me, too."

He chuckled, the sound warm and deep. "You're kidding. You'd rather have sanity than wild, crazy love?"

"You bet I would. I'm like you, Brett. I've seen what a supposed great love can do. There's Glory and Bowie. And what about my two big sisters? When Trista married Donny, she was so gone on him. She hung on his every word. It was Donny this and Donny that. He was the only man in the world. Now she's got three girls and Donny's hardly ever home. They have money problems. Same with Clarice. Her Mike was the great love of her life. Too bad they're always fighting now." Angie paused for a bite of cheesy potatoes. "And, well, look at me." She set her fork down and gestured, both hands out. "I always knew I wouldn't be like that, like my two big sisters, that I wouldn't go wild for some hopeless loser. But then along comes Jody with his Harley and his muscles and his bad attitude. And I went wilder than Tris and Risi put together."

Brett looked pleased. "You really do get it. You're with me on this."

She squared her shoulders and picked up her fork again. "You bet I am. I'm not going there again. After what happened with Jody, I just want to settle down— if I can find the right guy, I mean. Someone I can count on, someone I'll be proud to have count on me."

Brett said. "Yeah. That's it. That's what I want, too."

That night ended like the night before—with Nadine shooing them out at closing time. Brett walked Angie to the corner and she went home to the tiny cottage behind her mother's house, where she slept deep and dreamlessly, feeling safe and truly at home, as she hadn't since that awful day that Jody Sykes broke her heart and beat her black and blue.

The next night, it was the same. They closed up the clinic and headed for the Nugget where they talked and talked.

By Thursday night, it was getting to be a routine.

Brett said, "I have to tell you. It's the high point of the day for me. Us. Right here in our booth at the Nugget."

She said, "I know exactly what you mean. When we were kids, we never had much to say to each other…"

"Yeah. I was pretty shy."

"Me, too. But now…okay, it's sappy and I know it. But I feel like I can tell you anything. No subject is off limits. We can hash over whatever needs dealing with at the clinic. I can talk about what I want to do with my life. Whatever. Anything. It's all wide open, you know?"

"We can even be quiet together."

She nodded, grinning. And they were. Quiet. Neither of them said a word for five full minutes. And it was fine. Better than fine. It was comfortable. It was good.

Friday night, they slid into their usual seats and Nadine ambled over, propped her hip against the end of the booth and kidded, "So, you two, when's the wedding?"

It was a moment like the one when Glory's son was born. Angie looked across at Brett and he looked back at her….

And she *knew* they were thinking exactly the same thing.

He wanted a wife like her; she wanted a husband like him.

They felt safe with each other; they knew they could count on each other. They were friends from childhood, and over the past week they'd effortlessly become friends again—wait.

Scratch that.

They'd become *more* than friends: they were *best*

friends. They worked together and they *liked* working together. And after work, well, there they were, sitting across from each other in their favorite booth, talking for hours on end.

Best of all, what they felt for each other wasn't in the least wild or crazy or passionate. It was warm and friendly, trusting and good.

Brett asked her softly, "What do you say? We could go to Reno. Get a license, find a chapel…."

Angie didn't have to think twice. "I say yes."

He asked, again, carefully, "You're clear on this? You know what I'm asking you?"

"I am. And I do."

"I'm talking about right now. Tonight."

"Yes," she said once more, feeling strangely calm and utterly sure. "Let's go for it. Tonight."

They rose from the booth in unison.

"Wait a minute." Nadine had never sounded quite so stunned. "Is this for real?"

"Yeah," said Angie. "It's for real."

"Real as it gets." Brett got out his wallet and put a twenty on the table.

"Hey. Thanks." Nadine grabbed the bill and stuck it in her apron pocket. "And let me be the first to say…congratulations."

"We appreciate that." Brett reached out. Angie twined her fingers with his. Hand-in-hand, they headed for the door.

Chapter Three

The Reno marriage license office in the Washoe County Courthouse was open daily until midnight. Angie and Brett got there at a little before eight. They produced their drivers' licenses, answered a few basic questions, paid the thirty-five-dollar fee and received two copies of their marriage license—one to keep, and one for whoever married them to turn back into the courthouse within ten days of the ceremony.

Our marriage license, Angie thought. *Mine and Brett's. I can't believe it....*

They walked out of the courthouse and into a wedding chapel conveniently located right down the street. A plump fiftyish woman, her red hair teased and sprayed into an elaborate bouffant, greeted them at the door.

"I'm Marian." She beamed wide, displaying a mouthful of amazingly large white teeth, and put a chubby hand to her breast. "Welcome to the Sweetheart of Reno Wedding Chapel." The plump hand swept out. "We have all you'll need right here to make this blessed occasion one you'll remember always." She held up an index finger. "First, if I may suggest, a wedding gown? And for the groom, something a little more…festive? Let me show you what we have to offer in our Sweetheart Boutique."

Angie had no desire to spend a whole bunch of money on a spur-of-the-moment dress. "It's really not necessary."

But Marian either didn't hear her or pretended not to. She was already turning. "Right this way."

Angie glanced at Brett. He shrugged.

"Okay," said Angie. "I suppose it won't hurt to have a look…."

The boutique was off the reception area and packed with racks of white formals, some a froth of lace and tulle, some sleek and silky. There were other options: slim skirts and silk jackets with pretty beading; cocktail dresses. And for Brett, Marian offered a variety of tuxedos for rent. She had all the accessories, too: shoes and veils, beribboned garters, the works.

Angie was just slightly tempted—after all, they'd left the Flat without even stopping to think about clothes. Brett wore his usual khakis and a knit shirt. Angie had changed out of her nurse's tunic before they'd left the clinic, but otherwise she had on what she'd worn that morning: white jeans, a nondescript shirt and flat-soled shoes.

She fingered a froth of lace and peeked at the price tag: $2,569.99.

"It's your wedding," said Brett. "You should have a white dress." She tipped the price tag so he could see it. He didn't even flinch. "You want it? It's yours."

Now this, she thought, was a truly great guy. But they hadn't come to Reno to spend a small fortune on wedding clothes. Angie shook her head. "Not necessary. Let's just do it."

"At least choose a bouquet," he coaxed. The boutique had a refrigerated case full of them.

Oh, why not? She pointed at a ribbon-bedecked creation of yellow roses and white lilies. "How about that one?"

Marian took it out and handed it over with a flourish. "An excellent choice. A *perfect* choice."

Brett said, "And we'll need a ring."

Marian was only too happy to sell them one. Angie chose a simple gold band and insisted that Brett should have one to match.

"Now," said Marian, "as to the chapel. We have two. The Pink Chapel and the White. Let me show you the Pink first."

"White is fine," Angie decided right then. She'd never been real big on pink, anyway.

"Are you sure you wouldn't rather take a look at both options before making your final decision?"

Angie and Brett exchanged a glance. As if it mattered. The whole idea was to do this with no hassle and no fuss. They had no need for all the hoo-rah of a big wedding. They wanted a happy, normal life together and they were going to have one—starting tonight.

"We've decided," said Angie. "We'll take the White."

"Well, then." Marian beamed all the wider. "Right this way."

The White Chapel was truly, blindingly white: the walls, the ceiling, the floor, the simple altar that was really more like a podium. On either side of the altar, massive bouquets of artificial white hydrangeas exploded from tall white vases. A strip of plush white carpet served as an aisle between the rows of white wooden folding chairs.

"And here's Pastor Bob," announced Marian proudly as a big gray-haired fellow entered the all-white room.

"Greetings." Pastor Bob wore a black surplice and a royal-blue stole that made him look more like a late-in-life college graduate who had somehow misplaced his tasseled cap than any priest Angie had ever seen.

Priest....

The word got stuck in Angie's brain. Probably because she was a Dellazola and a cradle Catholic and Dellazola women *always* married in the church. Even her second sister, Clarice, who couldn't have a full mass because Mike wasn't a Catholic, had worn a big white dress and walked down the aisle of the New

Bethlehem Flat Catholic Church and stood before Father Delahunty to say her vows and receive the nuptial blessing….

Brett caught her hand and asked softly, "You doing okay?"

"Of course. Why?"

He gave her fingers a reassuring squeeze. "You look a little…doubtful, all of a sudden."

"Well, I'm not."

"You're sure?"

"I have never been so sure about anything in my entire life." And she honestly hadn't. The whole church-wedding issue was just one of those things her mother had drilled into her from birth, because when you were Catholic, getting married was nothing short of a calling from God. You couldn't just run off and do it. You were expected to get with a priest for nine months to a year in order to prepare yourself for such a sacred undertaking.

And in the Dellazola family, a huge reception always followed the church ceremony. Angie's parents had spent a small fortune on three weddings so far: Trista's, Clarice's and Dani's. Angie's mother, who knew how to pinch a penny until it screamed for mercy, kicked out all the stops when it came to her daughters getting married. She would spare no expense.

But this wasn't her mom's wedding, it was Angie's. And Brett's. They knew what they were doing and they didn't need a year of spiritual preparation—*or* a reception for a hundred, complete with sit-down, prime rib dinner. Uh-uh. They would be married this very night by a guy named Pastor Bob of indeterminate denomination, and that was all there was to it.

Pastor Bob said, "If the groom could stand here…" He pointed at the spot. Brett gave Angie's fingers one last comforting squeeze before he let go and moved to the place the pastor had indicated.

"If the bride will follow me…" Marian led the way down the white strip of carpet and out into the small foyer between the reception area and the chapel. Once they were beyond the chapel door, Miriam leaned close and spoke softly, as if imparting crucial and top-secret information. "I'm going to start the wedding march. Give it a few bars and then proceed at a stately pace toward your groom."

Brisk and still beaming, Marian trotted off. The familiar strains filled the air. Angie took her bouquet in both hands and stepped into position at the top of the plush white aisle.

Fifteen minutes later Angie and Brett climbed back into his Jeep Commander wearing their wedding rings. Angie turned to carefully lay her bouquet and their marriage license on the rear seat.

Brett glanced at his watch. "Well, it's a quarter of nine. I suppose we'd better figure out where to stay for our wedding night."

Wedding night.

Angie had one of those "Is this really happening?"

moments. Amazing, but true. They had done it. She and Brett were husband and wife.

He suggested, "How about Caesar's? It's only forty minutes or so to Tahoe. We can get a nice suite, have a little champagne.

A suite at Caesar's Palace. For a wedding night with Brett... She slid him a nervous glance.

He caught her looking and grinned. "Why am I getting the feeling that you're not quite ready to spend the night with me?"

She didn't know what to say. "Well, I'm sure that, um, making love with you is going to be...very nice...."

He actually chuckled. "You're scared."

"I am not—and anyway, we *are* married, so I guess I'd better get over my terror at the thought of seeing you naked...." Eeeuu. Now why had she said it *that* way? "Oops. Bad word choice."

He didn't look especially offended. "No kidding."

"But you know what?" She pulled her shoulders back and tried to look jokingly determined—at the same time ignoring the little curl of nerves that had tightened her tummy. "I'm ready, if you are."

"Interesting question..."

"What question?"

"Whether or not I'm ready. I'll have to think about that." He pretended to ponder—at length.

"Oh, stop." She punched him playfully in the shoulder. It was muscular, that shoulder. Like the rest of him. Now she actually thought about it, seeing him naked probably wouldn't be terrible in the least.

And one good thing had come out of the disaster with Jody. She'd had sex at last and found out that she really did like it. But with Brett? She simply had never considered such a thing—which was pretty dumb. After all, she'd just married the guy.

Brett stuck the key in the ignition and started the engine. "We're going home."

She grabbed his arm—which was warm and hard and dusted with dark hair. "No. Really. We should go to Caesar's."

"No. Really," he echoed, deadpan. "We shouldn't."

She threw up both hands and asked no one in particular, "Oh, why did I make such a big deal about this?"

He reached across and snared one her hands as she waved it in the air. "Because it *is* a big deal."

"But I—"

"You're not ready yet."

"How do you know if I'm ready or not?"

His looked at her patiently. "Angie…"

She grumbled, "I could *get* ready."

"Uh-uh. There's no rush. We're doing this *our* way, remember? We have every right to take our time."

He was right and she knew it. She looked down at their joined hands and then back up at him. "Okay. Like you said. There's no rush…"

He kissed her knuckles and then released her to shift into gear.

As the SUV pulled away from the curb, she cleared her throat. "Ahem. So. You never thought of *me* that way, either…did you?"

His gaze stayed focused on the stoplight ahead. "Sure, I did."

Too bizarre. She gulped. "You…you've thought of me naked?"

He smoothly braked as the light went red. "Angie. I'm a guy."

"Well, I know that."

"Thanks," he muttered dryly.

This was such a weird conversation. She should just shut up and let it be. But somehow she found herself opening her mouth again. "So…you *have?* You've thought of me naked? You really have?"

"Didn't I already answer that one?"

"Yeah. Yeah, I guess you did. I just can't believe it. You've thought of me naked…."

"And now that we're painfully clear on that, how about we move on to a fresh, new topic?"

"Uh. Sure. Of course. Yeah."

"You hungry?"

Now that he mentioned it, she was starved. "Good thinking. Let's eat."

Brett took his new bride to Monte Vigna at Atlantis for Italian. The food and the service were both great, as always. He watched her as she dug into her lobster ravioli and thought of that look she'd given him when he'd suggested they spend the night together at Caesar's. Priceless.

She glanced up from her plate. "What are you grinning about?"

"Not a thing."

Strange. Back when they were kids, she'd been sort of an honorary kid sister to him, someone he liked and looked out for and put up with. Back then, they were friends. Period.

But she'd filled out real nice in the years she'd been away, lost that angular, tomboy look she'd had in high school. And that first day he'd seen her again, when she'd come in for her interview at the clinic, he'd found himself noticing how much he'd liked the scent of her.

That was important, that a woman smelled good. And Angie did. She smelled like Ivory soap and sunshine. All clean and fresh and sweet.

No, it wasn't going to be any hardship for Brett to take his new wife to bed. But he did understand her hesitation. As logical and reasonable as their getting married was, it had happened pretty fast.

He had no problem with the idea of waiting until she was ready.

She glanced up from her food again and saw that he was still watching her. "Okay. What?"

"Eat your ravioli."

They were most of the way home when Angie remembered another important issue they'd yet to deal with. "Do you realize we haven't even talked about where we're going to live?"

He shrugged. "I suggest my place—unless you have something else in mind?"

She confessed, "I don't. Your place sounds just fine." Her stay in the cottage behind her mom's was only supposed to be temporary, anyway. The sooner she moved out, the sooner her folks could rent it again. Or maybe Glory would want to move in there with the baby. So far, Glory hadn't mentioned moving back to Chastity Bravo's B and B, where she'd worked as a maid until a few weeks before Johnny's birth. "Brett?"

"Yeah?"

"You know, I haven't even seen your place—I mean, not the inside." The day after Angie returned home, she and Glory had taken a long stroll around town. They'd walked past the house and Glory had told her that Brett lived there now.

He flicked a glance her way. His fine, dark eyes glinted with humor in the dashboard light. "You'll be seeing it soon—given that you're going to be living there."

"I always liked that house." Before Brett bought it, the house had belonged to a couple from the Bay Area who used it as a vacation home. "All those windows, and that big deck…"

"I think you'll like it there," he said. "I do."

"I'm sure I will. And do you think that maybe, um, tomorrow, you could borrow a pickup and—"

"I've got a pickup."

"You do?" She glanced his way again and saw that he was nodding. So strange. To be married to someone and not even know he had a pickup. "Well, then. You think we could move me in tomorrow?"

"Sure. Tomorrow's good. We can start early, get all your stuff moved in one day."

"There's not a whole lot. I sold most of my furniture before I moved home." She wondered how to say the next part without sounding as if she didn't want to be married to him, after all. She took a stab at it. "And maybe, for tonight…" How to go on?

He did it for her. "How about this? You go to your place for the rest of the night. First thing in the morning, you break the news to your family—being sure to remind them of all my sterling qualities. I want them greeting me with open arms when I show up with the truck to take you away from them."

She could have hugged him. "You understand." Which really shouldn't have surprised her. "But then, you always do." And the mention of breaking the news made her feel anxious all over again. "When I tell them, there will probably be shouting."

He slanted her a too-wise look. "Probably?"

She huffed out a breath. "You're right. I love my family, but we both know how they are. There *will* be shouting. There always is."

They were quiet again as the SUV rolled through the darkness, the sliver of moon overhead seeming to flicker on and off through the lacy, shadowed branches of the tall trees.

It was almost one when Brett pulled the SUV to a stop by the brick retaining wall in front of her mother's house. He turned off the engine. "Is ten tomorrow okay? Or do you think we should get started earlier?"

"Ten is good. The shouting might even be over by then." She reached between the seats and scooped up her bouquet. "I'll leave the marriage license with you, if that's okay?"

"No problem."

She smoothed the bouquet's trailing ribbons and then reached for the door handle. "Good night, Brett."

"Hey."

"Hmm?"

He leaned her way, one side of his mouth quirked up in a hint of a smile.

A kiss, she thought. Yes. That would be nice. She tipped her face up in invitation.

Their lips met. Like the kiss in the White Chapel that had sealed their vows, it was a light, tender kiss. A chaste kiss…

His lips were warm. Even after he pulled away, it seemed to her she could feel a tingling where his mouth had touched hers.

Chapter Four

Someone was knocking.

With a low groan of protest at being jarred from sleep, Angie rolled over in bed and squinted at the clock: 7:10. Bright morning light poured in through a gap in the curtains.

"Angie! Angela Marie…" Her mother's voice. Accompanied by yet more knocking.

"Ugh. Coming!" Angie dragged herself to a sitting position and lifted her hand to rake the tangled hair back off her face. The band of gold on her ring finger caught the light and twinkled at her. And she remembered….

The White Chapel. Marian and Pastor Bob. Brett holding her hand as she stood beside him at the altar….

"Angela!" That was Aunt Stella.

Time to face the music—or, in this case, the yelling and carrying on. "Coming, coming…" Angie shoved back the covers, grabbed her summer robe, stuck her feet in her floppy purple slippers and stumbled to the front door.

Her mother and her aunt stood close together on the step. Both wore wide, bright smiles. Too wide, maybe. And too bright…

Her mother held a bakery box. Aunt Stella clutched a big insulated carafe.

"We popped over to the bakery and brought those cheese Danish you like so much," said Rose.

"And coffee," Aunt Stella added, raising the carafe high.

Angie realized she was holding her left hand carefully out of sight on the other side of the open door. Talk about your futile gestures—and the whole point was to tell them this morning anyway.

Still, for the life of her, she couldn't bring herself to ease her hand around where her mom and aunt Stella might spot the ring on her finger. "What's this all about?" Angie couldn't help eyeing them with groggy suspicion. Coming over early with the coffee and the Danish wasn't the kind of thing her mom and aunt did every day. There was no special occasion that she could think of—well, okay. She'd gotten married last night. But *they* didn't know that.

Yet.

Did they?

"What's it *about?*" Mamma Rose repeated. She and Stella shared a meaningful glance. "Why, Angela Marie." Rose looked injured. "We bring Danish. And you ask what it's *about?*"

"And where are your manners?" Aunt Stella said it gently, but it was still a rebuke.

"Sorry…" Angie stepped back. "Come on in."

The two didn't need to be invited twice. They surged forward, sweeping past Angie, headed for her tiny kitchen. Not knowing what else to do, Angie shut the door and trailed along after them.

"Sit, sit." Her mother set the bakery box on the table and waved a hand toward one of the four fiddleback chairs. Angie sat. She also tucked her left hand under her thigh. She knew hiding her ring was pointless and cowardly and dumb. They would find out very soon anyway—at the very latest, by ten, when Brett showed up in his pickup to move her to his house.

Probably sooner than that—like in the next five minutes or so. Because it was going to get awkward trying to drink her coffee and eat her Danish with one hand tucked constantly out of sight. Her mom had sharp eyes and so did Aunt Stella. They'd notice that she wasn't using her left hand.

Still, Angie continued to sit on it. She watched her mother and her aunt bustle about. Rose was the taller of the two sisters. Aunt Stella was shorter and rounder. Rose kept her auburn hair free of gray with a little help from L'Oréal. Aunt Stella was letting her black hair go silver naturally.

For over a decade, the never-married Stella had lived in her sister's house and now the two worked effortlessly together in the small space, each knowing instinctively what the other would do, never once bumping into each other. Stella set the carafe on the table and got down a serving plate as Rose folded back the lid of the bakery box. Stella set down the plate and Rose transferred the Danish to it. Stella got out forks and small plates and mugs.

The sugar bowl was already on the table. Rose, looking for the milk, pulled open the door of the refrigerator before Angie remembered what she'd find in there.

"What's this?" Rose whirled. She had Angie's bridal bouquet in her hand and she brandished it like a deadly weapon.

Angie winced. "Oh. That. I stuck that in there last night. To keep it fresh, you know?"

For once, neither her mother nor her aunt said anything. They just stared at her. Waiting.

Until she finally confessed, "Okay. It's like this. It's my wedding bouquet."

Stella and Rose shared a stunned glance. Then they both gaped at Angie again. "Your *wedding* bouquet?" they echoed in unison.

"That's right." And why was she still sitting on her hand? No point in that now. She whipped it out from under her thigh and held it up. "Surprise," she said weakly, wiggling her fingers.

Stella gasped. "Angela Marie, that is a *ring* on your finger."

Angie gulped. "Yes, it is. Because you see, um, as it turns out…" She sucked in a fortifying breath and made herself come out with it—fast, so she wouldn't loose her nerve in the middle. "BrettandIgotmarriedlastnight."

"Married…" Her mother repeated the word much too softly.

Angie gulped again. "Yes. That's right. We got married."

There was another silence. It was huge.

Then Stella crossed herself. "Oh, Rosie. I knew it. Didn't I tell you? She's been out with him every night this week. The whole town's been talking. And the whole town is right."

Angie's mother set the bouquet on the table, sagged into a chair—and burst into tears.

"Shh, shh…" Stella wrapped an arm around her sister's shaking shoulders and frowned sternly at Angie. "Will you just look at your poor mamma…."

Angie felt exactly what her aunt intended her to feel: guilt. Bad-daughter guilt, to be specific. And as any daughter knows, that's the worst kind. "Mom. Look. I'm sorry. I know I should have said something, but—"

"Half the town knew." Stella stroked Rose's back and kept on as if Angie hadn't spoken. "But your own mamma? She didn't have a clue."

"Aunt Stella, I'm—"

"Don't start making excuses."

"I'm not, I'm only—"

"I hope you realize that Nadine's been telling everyone how she made a joke about wedding bells—and the two of you just got right up and headed for Reno."

"I'm sorry."

"A joke. You got married because Nadine Stout made a joke."

"No. That's not it. That's not it at all—and would you please stop yelling at me."

"I'm not yelling!"

"Yes, you are. And you're upsetting Mom."

"*I'm* upsetting her?"

"Yes." Angie rose. "You are."

"Well. Humph." But at least Stella shut up for a minute.

Angie got the box of Kleenex from the shelf. "Here you go, Mamma." Rose whipped one out and buried her face in it. "Mamma, listen…" Angie knelt by her mother's chair. "Brett's a good man. You know he is. Come on. Be happy for me…."

Rose heaved a quivering sigh. "I…just…don't believe it."

Stella scowled. "Back in town a week…"

"….and you've married one of the Bravo boys." Rose surrendered to a fresh flood of tears.

Angie patted her knee and waited.

Finally, Rose lifted her head and wiped at her eyes.

"I can't believe that one of my girls would run off and elope without even telling her own mamma that she's in love."

In love. Well, not exactly, Angie thought, but had the good sense not to say. "Mom, I mean it. I'm sorry. I should have told you. I realize that."

"And what about that big wedding you always wanted?" her mother loudly demanded with yet another sob. "What happened to that?"

"And," Aunt Stella hastened to add at a volume every bit as loud as her sister's. "What kind of marriage is it, anyway, if it's not in the church?"

"A *legal* marriage," Angie replied, quietly and with firmness.

"'Legal,'" Aunt Stella parroted. "'Legal, she says. For a good Catholic, legal isn't enough."

"She's right." Rose honked into her tissue. "Your aunt Stella is right." She started sobbing again.

It went downhill from there. As Rose sobbed, Aunt Stella alternately patted her back and lectured Angie on her thoughtlessness as a daughter and her terrible error in marrying outside the church. "Because a marriage in haste is no marriage at all," Aunt Stella declared. "Marriage is a *vocation,* a calling from God. It is not to be entered into lightly. It is a *sacrament,* permanent unto death, in which man and wife shall be faithful, each to the other—and, God willing, fruitful, as well."

Angie pressed her lips together and resisted the urge to ask her maiden aunt what made *her* such an expert on marriage. Uh-uh, better to let Stella rant and Mamma cry it out. They'd get used to the situation soon enough. The storm of tears and recriminations would blow over. Except for his not being Catholic—which was only any kind of obstacle for Aunt Stella anyway—Brett was excellent marriage material. Sure, he was a Bravo. But he was one of the *good* Bravos. He was settled, respected in town and gainfully employed.

Angie could have done a whole lot worse. And she had. Six months ago, in San Francisco—though that was a detail she wasn't sharing with her mamma or her aunt.

Eventually, Stella ran out of criticisms. Rose dried her eyes. "Well." Angie's mom let out a gusty sigh. "I suppose we might as well have our Danish."

So Angie took her bouquet off the table and Stella got the milk. Rose poured the coffee.

"It's really good," Angie said after she took her first bite. "Thank you."

Rose bravely sniffed and spoke to Stella. "See. She's a good girl at heart. She's polite."

"I never said she wasn't," Aunt Stella replied. She granted Angie a nod and reluctantly allowed, "You can have the marriage recognized. We'll arrange for a con-validation ceremony before Father Delahunty."

"And a big party after." Rose brightened at the thought. "Just like a real wedding reception. A nice dinner, with dancin' and a big, white cake…."

Stella sipped her coffee. "There's a waiting period,

though. Six months, I think. We'll have to talk to Father Delahunty."

Angie smiled and nodded and took another bite of Danish. If it made her mother happy, a big party was fine with her.

Rose said with a heavy sigh, "I suppose this means you'll be moving to Brett's house—and, wait a minute. What are you doing here, anyway? How come you didn't stay the night with your new husband?"

Because I wasn't quite ready for that, she thought. She said, "I wanted to have this little talk with you first." It was the truth, just not all of it. "So Brett and I agreed that I'd stay here at the cottage one more night...and yes. He's coming over with his pickup at ten."

Rose reached across and patted her hand. "Well. At least you married a man from town. You'll stay close to home for sure now, not be a stranger. I did worry about you, honey. All the way out there in the Bay Area, with no family close by."

"Well, you don't have to worry now, Mamma. I'm home to stay."

"It's nice, that pickup of Brett's," said Stella in a meditative tone. "New. One of those big, fancy Dodge Rams, with an extended cab..."

Rose looked up from her Danish. Her nose and eyes were red, but she was smiling. "And he *is* a doctor...."

By the time Brett showed up in his shiny new pickup, Rose and Stella were definitely looking on the bright side. They were also on the case, which meant they'd been on the phone, telling everyone in the family how Angie had run off to Reno with Brett Bravo.

Salvatore, Angie's younger brother, lived in L.A. Petra and Lucia, born between Dani and Glory, were away at school. Rose had called them and passed on the news.

Everyone else came rushing over. Tris and Risi brought their kids. Dani came with her husband, Ike. Anthony, the oldest of the Dellazola kids, showed up with his wife Gracie and their son, Baby Tony. Glory and five-day-old Johnny were already there, of course, as were Great-Grandpa Tony and Little Tony, Angie's dad.

The grandparents on the Dellazola side of the family, like Great-Grandpa Tony's wife, Maria, had passed on. But Nonna and Pop Baldovino, the grandparents on Rose and Stella's side, were still alive and kicking. They drove right over in their big old Lincoln Towncar.

The whole bunch ran out to greet the groom. There were hugs and kisses and a lot of back-slapping. Angie thought her new husband bore up pretty well under the flood of laughing, shouting Dellazolas and Baldovinos.

"Okay, now," said Angie's mom, once they'd all had a chance to welcome Brett into the family. "You pack Angie up and get her over to that beautiful house of yours. And then you both come back for lunch, you hear me, now?"

Brett promised that they would.

After that, most of the women headed for the kitchen, while the men helped Brett and Angie load up.

Angie's dad offered his truck and Anthony had his, too. Within an hour, they got all three pickups piled with everything Angie owned.

"There's a little more than I thought," she told Brett when she climbed into the passenger seat beside him. "Are you sure you have room for it all?"

"Don't worry. We have extra bedrooms on the lower floor. We can put all this stuff down there until we figure out how much we want to use."

We have extra bedrooms...

The way he said that melted her heart. He was generous, this new husband of hers. What he had, was hers.

She wished she had more to bring to the marriage, more to offer than just herself, a few thousand in savings and three pickups full of mismatched furniture and well-used household goods.

"What's that sad little look?" He had his arm draped on the back of her seat and he was leaning close, his eyes warm with concern.

"Just thinking I hope you didn't marry me for my money, because there isn't any."

He was shaking his head. "You kidding? I married you for your gorgeous face, those dimples and that hot body."

He was teasing—and yet his silly compliments made her feel better about not having more to bring to their life together. She answered him in kind. "Oh. Well, then. As long as you know what you're getting."

"I do. And I couldn't be happier about it."

Behind them, Anthony leaned on his horn.

Brett said, "Your brother's getting restless." He put the pickup in gear and off they went.

In the Flat—which was anything but—most of the houses were built on hillsides. Brett's place was no exception. The upper floor was the main floor, with extra bedrooms below. The main entrance faced the back and the hill behind it. A steep driveway led to the detached garage on the south side of the house. From the garage, a stone walkway curved to the door. When they got there, he unlocked it and pushed it wide—and then scooped her high against his chest.

"Welcome home, Angie." He carried her over the threshold into the open foyer.

She could see the living area beyond. It was one big, open space with a soaring cathedral ceiling and tall windows on three walls. French doors led out to the upper deck. Beyond the deck rail, a pair of stately firs framed the jutting black rocks across the river. Above the rocks, thick evergreens climbed the steep hillside.

"Oh, Brett. What a great place." She kissed him—a quick, firm peck on his warm, smooth-shaven cheek.

His eyes had never looked so soft, or so full of promise. "You can do better than that." He spoke low, his deep voice both tender and rough.

She felt the funniest, hollowed-out lurch in her stomach, a nervous little thrill.

Which was silly. It was just a kiss, after all. Only a kiss…

She gave his challenge back to him. "Try me."

So he did. He pressed his lips to hers, like last night—only better, somehow. His mouth was so soft and his arms, holding her, were so strong.

He kept the kiss light, just a tempting caress, a gentle press of his mouth to hers. She sighed as he brushed his lips back and forth on hers and found she could have kissed him for hours, held high in his arms in the open doorway of the house they would share from that day forward.

But then she heard heavy boots on the walk and Anthony grumbled in a joking tone, "Okay, you two. Knock it off. We've got work to do."

Brett whispered, "More later…" His breath was warm against her cheek.

"Definitely," she whispered back, a lovely feeling of anticipation blooming within her. "Much more." She giggled as he let her slide to her feet. "And I need a tour of my new home."

Anthony carried a big box of kitchen stuff. He bent to drop it on the step. As the pots and pans inside rattled and clanged, he muttered, "Work now, tour later."

"Oh, come on, Anthony," she wheedled. "Just a quick look around. Won't take a minute…"

Her big brother grumbled some more, but he made sure she saw him wink at her as he turned and strode back down the walk.

Brett showed her the bright, roomy kitchen area with its breakfast nook and acres of granite counters.

In the main room, she admired the formal dining area, the two separate groupings of sofas and chairs and the natural stone fireplace.

They proceeded to the master suite.

He had one of those platform beds. A really big one. She thought of the two of them, naked, in that bed.

It could happen tonight….

The idea still made her nervous. But then she remembered the warm, arousing feel of his lips against hers.

They'd do what came naturally.

It would be all right—not as wild and incredible as it had been with Jody. She didn't expect the earth to move or anything. But she wasn't in this for wild thrills. Uh-uh. In bed with Brett it would be…okay. *More* than okay. She was pretty sure of that now.

And Brett was watching her.

She slanted him a glance. "Nice bed," she said. "Really…big." He only grinned and gestured at the floor-to-ceiling windows and the second set of French doors leading out to the deck.

He led her through the pair of walk-in closets and on to the gorgeous bath, which had his-and-hers sinks, glass-block windows, a giant tub and an open-front shower.

"This way," he said as they left the master suite. They went down the stairs to another central living area off of which branched three more bedrooms, two baths and a laundry room. There were French doors down there, too, opening onto a brick patio covered by the deck above.

Brett kissed her again before they went back up to the main floor. He touched her cheek, stroked her hair and trailed a warm finger down the side of her throat.

She shivered a little in the wake of his touch. It was good.

Better than good.

When he stepped back, he smiled at her. "We should go up. Your brother will start getting impatient."

"He was just teasing."

"I know. But it's not fair that he and your dad should have to do all the work." He held out his hand. She laid hers in it and he led her to the stairs.

Back at the Dellazola house an hour later, lunch was on the table—or, to be more specific, several tables pushed together in the big family dining room. Old Tony broke out the elderberry wine and there were toasts: to love, to happiness, to a dozen baby Bravos...

Brett enjoyed himself immensely. He'd always liked the Dellazolas. You knew where you stood with folks like them. And they were pleased, every last dark-eyed, dimple-cheeked one of them, about the marriage. They were pleased and they said so. Brett appreciated that.

He and Angie held hands under the table—as corny and romantic as a couple of newlyweds. Which, come to think of it, they were. Now and then they would share a glance and she would give him that special smile....

He was looking forward to getting her alone.

Tonight would be their first real night together as husband and wife. He wasn't going to rush her.

But, as he'd reminded her last night on the way home from Reno, he *was* a guy. And she was a pretty woman who smelled good and felt even better when he held her in his arms.

A pretty woman who just happened to be his wife.

"Oh, man…" Across the table, Anthony was grinning and shaking his head.

Brett frowned. "What?"

"Nice to see, that's all. You and Angie. Husband and wife…"

"Love is a beautiful thing," said Anthony's wife, Gracie, leaning toward her husband and planting a kiss on his bearded cheek.

And that got Old Tony going again. "To love. To love. Let's drink to love…."

Brett wasn't in love. And neither was Angie. But he figured that was something nobody else needed to know. He picked up his glass and raised it high. "To love…"

The two words echoed down the table. "To love…"

"To love…"

"To love…"

"To love…"

Even the little kids at the low table in the corner raised their glasses of grape juice and echoed the toast.

About then, Mamma Rose began to cry—from happiness, she said. And the religious one, Aunt Stella, started in about how he and Angie would need to "rectify their unfortunate choice" of not getting married in the church. "You must speak with Father Delahunty," Stella instructed. "Find out what the waiting period will be. And, Dr. Brett, I want you to seriously consider converting to the Catholic fai—"

"Put a sock in it, Aunt Stella." Anthony cut her off. "It's not the time."

Mamma Rose sniffed and dabbed her streaming eyes. "Anthony." The word was freighted with reproach.

"Sorry, Aunt Stella," Anthony muttered. "But save it for later, okay?"

Stella pinched up her mouth, but she did keep it shut.

Old Tony—who was definitely on his way to getting blasted on his own homemade wine—raised his glass for yet another toast.

But before he could get a word out, Trista put up a hand and cried, "Wait! Wait a minute. Stephanie? Where's Steffie?" Stephanie was her youngest, just two.

Everyone looked toward the low table in the corner where the kids too small for the main table but old enough to be out of high chairs, sat together. One small seat was empty.

"Lulu," Trista spoke sharply to her oldest. "I told you to watch her."

Lulu hitched up her small chin. "She said she had to go potty. I *told* her I'd help her. She stuck out her tongue at me. You know how she gets. She said she was a big girl and she could do it herself."

"Tris, it's okay." Clarice tried to soothe her sister. "She can't have gone far."

Trista wasn't listening. She'd already leaped to her feet and headed for the door. Clarice got up and followed her.

The second the two women were out of sight, Old Tony tapped his glass with his fork. "Okay, now. Where was I?" He held his glass high. "To our Angie's new husband. Brett, welcome to our family."

Brett nodded his thanks and they all drank again— by then, most of them, including Brett and Angie, were toasting with water.

Once that toast was over, Pop Baldovino launched into a long story about how he'd courted his wife and won her away from a rich Nevada City Irishman. He was just to the part where she told him yes, when Trista came flying back into the room, face white as a fresh strip of surgical gauze, Clarice at her heels.

"We can't find her anywhere," Trista cried. "She's gone. My baby's just…gone."

Everybody jumped up from the table and pitched in to look for the missing toddler. They fanned out, some scouring the lower floor, some heading upstairs to check all the bedrooms, a few racing for the basement to see if little Steffie might have stumbled down there.

When she didn't turn up in the house, the family poured out onto the front lawn and the terraced garden in back. Trista ran down the brick steps to the street, calling, "Steffie, where are you? Steffie, my God!" Clarice had to chase after her and calm her down.

They checked the cottage, scouring every room.

No sign of the little girl.

By then, poor Trista was nothing short of a wreck. She clung to Clarice, sobbing, "Oh, I should have watched her closer. Oh, I can't believe she's gone."

Most of the women gathered in the living room to comfort Trista and to reassure her that her baby would be found. The men continued looking, in the house and outside. Brett wandered out to the front hallway and tried to come up with any places they might have forgotten to check.

He treated a lot of toddlers at the clinic, Stephanie included. Kids that age seemed to like cozy spaces where bigger folks couldn't go—cozy places like maybe that door under the stairs.

The door was three feet high, max, at its tallest point, tucked back in the shadows and slanted to follow the rise of the stairs. Brett had to crouch and scoot under there to get to it. He grabbed the porcelain knob and pulled it open.

Sure enough, there she was, sound asleep, her small head resting on a dog-eared stuffed bunny, sucking her thumb. As the light from the hallway touched her round, pink cheek, she opened her eyes.

The thumb popped free of her mouth and she frowned at him, befuddled in the cutest, little-kid way. "Docca Bwett?"

He gave her a slow smile. "Steffie. We've been looking all over for you."

She sat up, grabbed her stuffed bunny and held out her soft little arms. "I go potty. All by myself. Then I get *vewwy* tired…"

He scooped her close. She wrapped her arms around his neck, the bunny dangling from her small hand. He felt the ragged stuffed toy plop against his back and he thought how great it was going to be when he and Angie had some kids. He wanted a little girl first. Hell. On second thought, he didn't care.

A boy or a girl. Either. Both….

He ducked out from under the stairs, Steffie clinging to his neck. Rising to his height, he turned toward the door to the living room.

Rose spotted him first. She let out a joyful cry. "Here she is! Brett's found her!"

And everybody jumped up and rushed over to surround him and Stephanie. They all pressed in, jostling each other, yet still somehow managing to clear a path so Trista could get through.

"Mommy, Mommy, I was *sweeping*…" Steffie swayed toward her mother.

Trista caught her and cuddled her close. "Oh, my baby, my baby, you're all right…." Trista stroked her daughter's silky hair and gazed up at him gratefully, brown eyes brimming. "Thank you, Brett. Oh, thank you, thank you…"

Cool, soft fingers sought his. Angie. He turned and she was grinning at him. "Our hero," she said in a tone both teasing and tender, as everyone clapped his shoulders and patted him on the back.

It wasn't a bad moment, Brett thought as he bent his head to press a quick kiss on the sweet, upturned lips of his bride. Not a bad moment at all.

He had what he wanted now—what he needed. A good woman with a level head and a ready smile. They would share a sane life, serving their community, raising children who would grow up safe and loved and confident in the reasonable, settled *normalness* of their parents and their world.

Chapter Five

They didn't get away from the party until after three. The family followed them outside, some of them trailing down the brick steps, others remaining up on the lawn, everybody waving and calling out good wishes as Angie and Brett headed off down the street on foot.

It was a warm, clear day, perfect for a stroll, so earlier they'd left Brett's fancy pickup at home and caught a ride back with Anthony.

Home…

Angie smiled to herself. Her own home at last. With Brett.

Hard to believe that a few short weeks ago she'd

been in despair, wondering how she could have chosen so badly, how her life could have gone so very wrong. Now, everything was changed. She was married to a wonderful guy and things had never seemed so right.

She tipped her head to the clear sky above, thankful for the warmth of the sun on her face—not to mention to be settled at last in her hometown, with a man she trusted and respected by her side.

The Sierra Star Bed-and-Breakfast loomed ahead as they reached the intersection where Jewel Street dead-ended into Commerce Lane. A rambling clapboard building painted a cheery yellow, the B and B had a white picket fence in front and a slate walk leading up to the front porch.

"We should stop and say hi," Angie suggested, "and we need to tell your mom the news."

Brett made a low sound. "As if she doesn't already know by now."

"All the more reason to drop in—because she's family and she should have heard it from us…."

He lifted their clasped hands and brushed a kiss across her knuckles, causing a lovely warmth to flare down low inside her. "Are you talking about *my* mom—or yours?"

"Oh, Brett…" She swayed toward him. He gathered her close, right there in the street. So what if folks saw them and talked? They were newlyweds, after all. And newlyweds were allowed the occasional public display of affection. She tipped her face up to him. "You amaze me. How do you understand me so well?"

He touched her—a breath of a touch, warm fingers skimming under her chin, down her cheek. "You did have that look."

"What look?"

"Kind of guilty, maybe?" His body felt good—warm and strong, hard where hers was soft.

Funny, but every time he touched her, it was better than the time before—and what were they talking about? Oh, yeah. Guilt. "I'm not feeling guilty…"

He grinned. "The hell you're not."

'Well. Not *too* guilty, anyway."

"It was rough, telling your mom?"

"What can I say? There was crying and yelling. Nothing new about that. And then, in the end, she came around."

"Whew."

"You have her full approval. She likes you. She always has. My dad likes you, too. Plus, you're a doctor with a brand-new pickup and a nice house. I'd have to say, you're about the perfect man in every way. Well, I mean, other than not being Catholic."

"Sorry about that."

"Oh, and you will be much sorrier, believe me. Once my aunt Stella gets through with you—though I swear I'll do all I can to protect you."

"That's something, at least…" His gaze tracked to her mouth.

And then he lowered those tempting lips and he kissed her. Right there, in the middle of Jewel Street, with the sun pouring down on them, out in the open where anyone could see.

She kissed him back. It was a great kiss and she never wanted it to end.

But eventually he lifted his head and she looked in those dark eyes and…

Oh, for the night to come. By then, Angie had no doubts at all. It was going to be great, making love with her husband. As a matter of fact, she could hardly wait.

With a happy laugh, she danced back, out of the cherishing circle of his arms, catching his hand and giving it a tug. "Now come on. Let's go see *your* mom."

Tall and slim with a tidy cap of short, gray-streaked brown hair, Chastity emerged from the house as they let themselves in the gate.

"Well. It's about time you two got over here and let me congratulate you." She reached for Angie first. "Come on. I want to hug my new daughter-in-law." Angie moved forward into Chastity's embrace. "I'm so happy." Chastity squeezed Angie tight, then took her by the shoulders and held her away. "I confess, I've always hoped that someday you two might get together, ever since those long-ago days when you and Brett were constantly trooping in and out of here, getting mud all over my hardwood floors…."

Chastity turned to her son, who swept her up into his big, strong arms for a hug of his own.

When he finally let her go, she commanded, "Come

on inside, you two. I baked a chocolate cake this morning and I've got a fresh pot of coffee brewing."

In Chastity's kitchen at the back of the B and B, Brett and Angie filled her in on all the details of their Reno wedding and got the latest on how Buck and his wife were doing in New York. Chastity also said that Glory would be moving back to the Sierra Star next week.

"I'll help her out with the baby." The lines around Chastity's mouth deepened with her pleased smile. "I'm looking forward to getting to know my new grandson a little." She didn't say that Glory couldn't wait to get out from under the disapproving eyes of the family, but Angie knew that must be the case. Pretty much everyone—from Mamma to Aunt Stella, to Great-Grandpa Tony—thought that Glory should go ahead and marry Bowie for the sake of little Johnny. They all felt Bowie would settle down once Glory finally became his wife. And none of them ever kept their feelings to themselves. By now, Glory had to be getting pretty sick of being stuck at Mamma's house, where everyone was only to happy to tell her how to live her life.

Angie was the only one in the family who saw things from Glory's perspective: a guy with problems was a guy with problems, whether he was married or not. Glory counted on Angie's support. In the past week, since Angie had started spending all her free time with Brett, she knew she'd neglected Glory.

Tomorrow, Angie promised herself, she'd get over

to the house and spend some quality time with her little sister.

But for today—and the night to come…

Well, she *was* a newlywed. She wanted to be with her groom.

At the house by the river, just the two of them, at last, they sat out on the deck together. The trees rustled in the wind overhead and the river made that soft, constant sigh of sound as it tumbled through the canyon a hundred yards away. They laughed over the antics of her crazy family and marveled some more about all the things they had in common. They both read *The Week* magazine. They had the same favorite color, turquoise. He liked action movies—so did she.

"As long there's a love story," she qualified.

He groaned, but then he nodded. "Okay. I can live with the mushy stuff, in moderation."

They even talked about children.

"I'm up for two," she told him, thinking of her family. She loved them all, couldn't imagine a world without each and every one of them in it. But growing up, she'd often felt just a little bit ignored, a quiet middle child in a rambunctious crowd of nine. "I mean, if more come along, of course, I'll adore them. But with two, we can be sure each one gets lots of attention."

Brett agreed. "Two it is—and you're grinning. Why?"

"Just remembering what it was like growing up in a

big family. Looking back, I'd have to say that today was the most attention I've gotten from all of them since my first communion." She laughed. "And no. I'm not complaining. As a rule, my family's undivided attention is the *last* thing any smart girl would ever want. I mean, look at poor Glory. They all want her to marry Bowie and they'll never leave her alone until she does."

Brett was shaking his head. "But it's *her* decision."

"Tell that to my great-grandpa Tony."

He suggested, "What do you say to holding off on the kids for a while? I want you to myself for a year or two. And then, there's the clinic. We're just getting started there. I'd like us to have some time to get more established."

"I think you're right. We need some time for just the two of us." Babies were a blessing, but they were also a challenge. They put any number of stresses on a marriage.

"A full year," he bargained. "Before we start trying for kids. Will that work for you?"

She was in total agreement. "That's perfect for me." Since she was wary of the pill and its side effects, she made a mental note to get a new diaphragm—and ignored the familiar twinge of guilt that accompanied the thought. No, Aunt Stella would not approve. Neither would Father Delahunty.

But this was Angie's life—hers and Brett's. And they both agreed they needed a little time to themselves before the kids came along.

Back inside, they spent an hour or so unpacking and putting away the things Angie was sure she would need. The rest, they left down in one of the spare rooms to deal with later. She did get out a few treasures—a shepherd-boy Hummel figurine left to her by her granny Dellazola, a sleek green cloisonné vase and a pink-hearted conch shell she'd bought on a trip to Malibu. She asked Brett if she could set them around.

"Your house, too," he reminded her.

"I knew you'd say that."

"Then why did you ask?"

"Because I wanted to hear it. *My house, too.* Oh, yeah. I like the way that sounds." She stepped up close and kissed him, quick and hard. "I think the shell would look beautiful on that glass table by the French doors…." She started to turn.

He caught her arm. "Do that again." He pulled her closer—so close she could see the gold flecks in his dark eyes, flecks so small, they were invisible from any distance, flecks like the tiny specks of gold dust that could be found, now and then, sparkling bright in a handful of river sand.

Oh, and she did like the scent of him. He smelled of fresh air and clean skin, with just a hint of some nice, mellow aftershave—and something else, too. Something indefinable, but definitely male.

She marveled how everything about him, each little detail, pleased her so thoroughly. How could it have taken her so long—all her life, until today—to realize she desired him?

"Do what again?" she asked, as if she didn't know.

"Kiss me."

She lifted her mouth to him. His lips touched hers and his arms closed around her.

Oh, he did feel good: the softness of his mouth, the strength in his arms, the hardness of his lean body, and its warmth. She put her hands on his big shoulders, just to felt the muscular shape of them.

He deepened the kiss. His tongue touched the seam where her lips met. With a hungry cry, she slid her arms around his neck and let him in.

Oh, the sheer pleasure of it—the velvety roughness of his tongue as it stroked past her parted lips and found the slick, wet surfaces inside. Angie gasped, instinctively pressing her hips up to him, feeling him *there* for the first time, her body catching fire at the intimate contact.

His big hands splayed on her back and he pressed her ever tighter into him. She reveled in that, in how tightly he held her, in the strong thrusting of his tongue in her mouth, in the low, needful moan that rose from his throat.

A miracle.

She *wanted* him. Wanted Brett. Her lifelong friend, and now, so suddenly, her husband. She wanted him—and he wanted her.

He took the hem of her snug red T-shirt and yanked it upward. The kiss broke—just long enough that he could whip that shirt off and away—and his mouth covered hers again.

A groan of sheer delight escaped her as he cupped her breasts. He groaned, too. Even with the barrier of her lacy bra between his warm palms and her aching flesh, the sensation was electric.

She slid her hand down between them, to touch him, curling her fingers over the hard, thick length of him beneath his clothes, groaning again at the sheer wonder of it, of touching him, of having him touch her.

She couldn't wait any longer.

She needed him, had to have him.

He must have felt the same, because all at once they were tearing at each other's clothes. She undid his khakis and shoved them down, along with the boxers beneath. A flick of his clever fingers and her bra came undone. She wiggled it off and tossed it over her shoulder.

They let go of each other—long enough to step back and get out of their shoes, their socks, her jeans, his collared knit shirt. Within seconds, they were both naked, standing there in the middle of the great room, revealed to each other in the afternoon light....

Angie's heart thrummed a hot tattoo under her breasts just to look at him.

If a man could be called beautiful, Brett was, with those broad shoulders and leanly muscled arms, his tapering waist, tight belly and hard thighs. Her breath all tangled in her throat, wet and yearning down below, she glanced up, into those gold-flecked dark eyes—and then down again, her gaze lingering on the thick, jutting evidence that he wanted her every bit as much as she wanted him.

She really, truly hadn't expected this…this burning. This need. This feeling that she might die if she couldn't have this man—her husband—inside her, right now.

"Oh, Brett…" Her throat clutched. She gulped to ease the sudden tightness, licked her lips in anticipation.

And faintly, from somewhere outside, she heard a woman's voice calling, "Jimmy, come on home. It's dinnertime…"

The windows…

Through the humid fog of overwhelming desire, it came to her that they were standing stark-naked in the middle of the great room, surrounded by windows with all the blinds wide open.

Anyone who happened to look in might see them….

Her lust-dazed mind skittered away from the thought. Really, it *was* still daylight and none of the lamps in the room were on. With the brighter light outside, the windows would be opaque to anyone strolling by on the street.

Wouldn't they?

Brett realized the problem, too. But he didn't agonize over it. He only said, low and roughly, "Angie. You're beautiful. And I think we'd better shut the damn blinds…."

She laughed then, a giddy laugh that seemed to shimmer through her, warm as sunlight, bright as a new day. Had a woman ever been so happy as she was at this moment? So desperate for the touch of a certain special man—and yet, at the same time, so completely fulfilled?

Her whole body was aching for him. But in her heart, she'd never felt so light, so sure.

And he was right. They'd better get the blinds closed.

They raced around the big room in their birthday suits, pulling the cords on all the blinds, leaving them slanted just enough to give them light to see by.

Brett shut the last blind and turned to her. He held out his hand. "Come here." Again, his voice was rough and low. Tempting her.

Commanding her…

Heat flooded her, a wash of yearning so powerful she felt weak with it. And somewhere far back in her mind, a warning bell sounded.

How could this be happening with Brett? It wasn't supposed to be this way. Not with Brett.

This feeling wasn't…safe. The wild pulsing of her blood, the weakness in her knees, the heavy wetness between her legs, the overwhelming ache in every cell of her body—to touch him. To take him inside her…

This was stronger. More powerful. More consuming than anything she'd ever felt before.

This made all the hot times with Jody seem…what?

The word came to her. Shallow. Yes. Shallow and trivial—less than a pale imitation…of this.

This, which was turning out to be a lot more than she'd ever expected.

This, which was a far cry from what she and Brett had agreed on.

This, which was everything wild and crazy and out of control—all that stuff she and Brett had supposedly married to avoid.

Well, and so what?

She almost laughed again—for sheer joy. It appeared she was going to get more than she'd ever imagined in this marriage. It appeared she was going to have great sex—the *best* sex of her life. Tonight.

With her husband.

And really, did she have a problem with that?

She felt the slow, knowing smile as it curved her lips.

"Angie. Come here." He started toward her, the fine muscles in his strong legs bunching with each step, his desire for her standing out proud.

She didn't have to be told a third time. Head up and shoulders back, she crossed the wide room to meet him halfway.

When she stood before him, she put her hand in his.

He reeled her in.

Bending his head to hers, he covered her mouth in a hard, potent kiss, his tongue pushing in, sweeping over her teeth, flicking the roof of her mouth, until she moaned and rubbed her breasts against his chest, so her nipples drew up all the tighter.

He brought his hands between them and cupped her

breasts, catching the nipples and rolling them, making them ache deliciously, causing her blood to thicken in her veins and her breath to snag high in her chest.

Below, she felt herself opening, wetter than ever, aching for the feel of him…

He cradled her face in cherishing hands and he went on kissing her in that demanding, arousing way, his fingers easing up under her hair and then combing down through the loose strands. He trailed a finger along her spine, tracing each bump, moving lower, until he cupped her bottom and pulled her to him— tighter.

Harder.

He let one hand trail upward, as, with the other, he held her firmly in place, pressing her against his raging erection. He traced a squiggly pattern on her flesh, one that left hot little flares of intense sensation as that taunting finger moved up, into the curve of her lower back and over, down the side of her hip…

And inward.

She cried out, into his mouth. He thrust his tongue deeper, moaning. She drank that sound.

And he had loosened his hold on her bottom just enough that he could slip that wandering hand of his between them. He found the thatch of moist curls, the slickness beneath. Angie shuddered.

He caught her lower lip between his teeth, worried it gently, murmured into her mouth, "So hot, so wet…for me…"

She moaned in response. "Yes. Oh, yes…"

And he delved in, stroking her, slipping a finger deep inside, and then two, sliding them, in and out, in a rhythm so slow and sweet it drove her wild.

Wild…

Oh, yeah.

She wasn't supposed to be wild for her husband. That wasn't the plan.

But too bad for the plan.

She was wild for Brett—in a purely sexual way.

Not love, she promised herself. She wasn't in love. But in *lust?* Oh, yeah.

And it felt fine. Better than fine. A thousand times better. She moved her hips in time to the strokes of his knowing hand and felt her body readying, rising toward the finish….

And then, just before she went shimmering on over the edge of the universe, he stopped—but only long enough to take both her hips in his big hands and lift her.

She let out a moan that went on forever as she locked her legs around him and she felt him—nudging her slickness, inching inside, stretching her in the most perfect, thrilling way.

Oh, he felt so good, better than anything she'd ever felt before.

He groaned. "Hold on…"

And she did, with a pleasured little whimper, as he carried her, wrapped tight around him, to a section of wall by the door to the master suite.

He backed her up to it, so she could brace herself. She let her head drop back against that wall and opened her eyes to lazy slits.

"Feels...so good. So good. Oh, Brett..." She reached out, traced the shape of his ear, touched his thick, close-cropped hair. The ends were blunt against her stroking fingers. She pulled him close, whispered again, "Oh, Brett..."

And that was when he began to move. Cradling her hips, holding her in place, he retreated and then slowly entered once more....

She canted back from him, using the wall for balance, wrapping her legs more firmly around him, hooking her feet together, so she could better aid him. Her body took its cues from his, lifting when he retreated, settling as he came into her again.

"Beautiful," he muttered, the word deep and raw, elemental, stripped down to its purest form. "Beautiful..." His fingers, curving to hold her from below, stroked her, opening her, from underneath, touching her most secret places as he pushed in and withdrew. "Watch," he whispered, bending his head to hers, catching her earlobe between his teeth, licking it as he whispered again, "Watch..."

So she watched, her body heating to fever pitch at the sight of him, thick and hard, roped with blue veins and slick with her wetness—thrusting in, gliding out, sliding in again, until her mound pressed tight against his lower belly, so close, so...connected.

Oh, she had truly never, ever felt like this before.

And she was rising again, her body tightening around him, every nerve singing, the blood rushing to her center. Her legs shook with the force of it and she drew him closer, wrapping her arms around his neck, holding tight so she wouldn't fall.

The sweet contractions started, her body milking its pleasure from his. He moaned low and she felt him, going over with her, thrusting so deep, pinning her hard against the wall.

They were completely still on the outside, exploding within, holding each other so tight, their bodies straining and slick with sweat. He groaned, a sound dredged up from the depths of him, and he buried his head in her shoulder, nipping her flesh, drawing the tender spot against his teeth, licking as he sucked.

"Yes," she moaned, and, "Yes," again. "Like that. Oh, Brett. Like that…"

He kissed the spot he'd sucked. "Angie…" He made her name sound like a prayer.

The pulsing went on and on—his. Hers.

It was all one—*they* were one. She contracted around him and he spilled into her. The achingly beautiful sensation rippled out along every nerve, until, clutching him close, she tossed her head against the wall, crying out her completion—and finally, so softly, whispering his name.

Chapter Six

After that first time, they couldn't keep their hands off each other.

Brett wondered at the whole situation—a little.

But not a lot. What red-blooded man would?

On the spur of the moment, he'd headed for Reno and married his best friend, his sidekick, the girl next door—and discovered that she also just happened to be his sexual dream girl. How often did that happen?

Brett didn't know. Hell, he didn't especially care. Angie wanted him and he damn well wanted her. It was a nice extra bonus to what was clearly the best choice he'd ever made in his life—spur of the moment or otherwise.

Okay, in that first, hot, incredible weekend of their marriage, they weren't as careful as they should have been, given their agreement to hold off on kids for a while.

But he did have condoms and they did use them. Just not quite all the time.

That first evening, as daylight faded beyond the bathroom's glass-block windows, they took a bath together. He turned on the air jets so she could have bubbles—and the massaging jets, too, just for the hell of it. They floated around in the high, white, pulsing froth, laughing, kissing, pausing to indulge in a lingering touch.

She wrapped her soft fingers around him. He groaned as the pleasure sliced through him, hot and sweet. She kissed him, with the steam rising around them, her soft brown hair, which she'd pinned up loosely, tumbling in little corkscrew curls around her moist cheeks. The taste of her was like no woman he'd ever known. He lay back in the foaming water and let those fingers of hers have their way with him.

Later—much later—they turned on the lights in the great room and headed for the kitchen to whip up a little midnight snack. In an unnecessary nod to modesty, she'd pulled on his knit shirt. He'd put on his boxers.

Five minutes later the shirt was dangling off the back of a chair and the boxers were hanging from the refrigerator. Angie, gorgeously naked, sat on the granite peninsula with her long, slim legs around his waist and her slender arms braced on his shoulders.

She amazed him, astounded him, stole his breath right clean away.

He bent over her, there on the counter, and he took one hard, dusky-pink nipple in his mouth. She groaned low and ground her hips against him, lifting her torso, so he could have more.

Amazing. Oh, yeah. That was the word for her.

Once he let her down off the counter, she put his shirt back on, washed her hands and whipped them up a couple of omelets. He made the toast.

They ate. Then came the best part: they went to bed.

They lay under the covers, with the light of the almost full moon shining silver in the windows and they whispered to each other, of hopes.

Of dreams.

Of what might come to be.

Of what they absolutely *would* make happen.

He kissed her slowly, caressing her, exploring all her sleek, soft hollows, her rounded, inviting curves. He pushed the covers down and he looked at her, silvered in moonlight. Never had he seen such a beautiful sight. He told her so. She reached up her arms to him.

"Not yet," he whispered. He put his mouth to the hollow between her breasts, that vulnerable spot just beneath the place where her ribs met. He stuck out his tongue and he tasted her—the sweet and the salt of her. He laid his head there, in that warm, smooth hollow.

Her arms came around him, holding him, and he listened to the rhythm of her heart.

But not for long. Soon, he was kissing her again, trailing his tongue downward, dipping into her navel, sliding over, to trace wet circles on the jut of a hipbone, to track the tender line where her thigh met her body.

He made her moan. He really liked that: hearing Angie moan. He nuzzled the dark curls that covered her sex and then he parted them—first with a teasing finger. Then with his mouth.

She gave herself up to him, crying out and clutching the sheets, her body bowing up, her smooth thighs spread wide for him. When she reached her peak, he slid up her body. She was open for him, ready—and so wet, she took him in one easy, deep glide.

He looked down into her wide, soft brown eyes as they moved together. "Beautiful," he whispered.

She held up her mouth to him. He kissed her, spearing his tongue in, groaning as he came.

In the morning she spoke of going to see Glory. But somehow she never quite got out the door.

A look, or a brushing touch. That was all it seemed to take with them. He would look at her. She would let out a soft sigh.

And he'd have to reach for her, have to press his lips to hers and pull that gorgeous body close.

They joked that there wasn't a surface they couldn't make love on. No counter or piece of furniture was too small or too uncomfortable: the sofas, the chairs, the kitchen and bathroom counters, the washer in the laundry room downstairs—the dryer, too.

Sunday night, late, as they were settling into their bed, he got an emergency call. Angie volunteered to go with him. But he cupped her sweet face in his hands and kissed her. "Stay here. No reason for both of us to go."

"You sure?"

"I'm sure. Keep the bed warm. I'll be home before you know it...."

Not exactly.

It was after three when he eased into bed beside his sleeping wife. She sighed as he gathered her close. He kissed the satiny crown of her head and stared at the moon out the window and thought that he was the luckiest man on the face of the earth.

Monday morning, Angie stole a moment from the rush to get ready for work and gave her baby sister a call. Since Glory was still at their mother's, Angie had to get past whoever answered the phone first. That turned out to be Great-Grandpa Tony.

"Angie!" the old man crowed. "How you doin' in that fine, new house of yours?"

"I love it here, Grandpa."

"How's married life treatin' you?"

"It's great. Is Glory there?"

The old man made a snorting, disapproving sound.

"Now, where else would she be—since she refuses to marry the father of her baby? I tell you, Angie. It ain't right. That little baby deserves—"

"Grandpa?"

"Eh?" More snorting and grunting. "What?"

"Could you just put Glory on?"

"Young people. Always in such a big damn rush." Judging by the clattering sound that came next, Old Tony had dropped the phone—probably in disgust. "Glory!" Angie heard him shout. "Glory, it's the phone!"

A moment later Angie heard a click as Glory picked up an extension. "Hello?"

"Hey, there. It's me. How 'bout lunch? Eleven-thirty, at the diner?"

"You can't possibly know how much I would love that. I'll be there. You're buying."

"Whatever it takes."

Someone snorted. "Angie, you talk to her." Great-Grandpa Tony was back on the line. "Make her see the light."

Glory made a low, growling sound. "And they all wonder why I can't wait to get out of here."

Dixie's Diner had stood on Main Street across from the grocery store for as long as Angie could remember. According to town legend, there *had* once been a Dixie, back before World War II. But she was long gone.

Angie arrived right on time for her lunch with Glory. Even at eleven-thirty, the long counter with its chrome-

and-red-vinyl stools was full. As were half the center tables and all of the booths. Luckily, Glory had gotten there early. She waved from the back booth and Angie hurried to join her.

Currently, the diner was owned and run by Charlene Cooper, who'd been a year behind Angie in school and who'd inherited the place when her mom and dad died. Charlene had been barely eighteen when the tragedy occurred. The Coopers had gone off the road and into the river far below.

Angie was just sliding into the booth opposite Glory when Charlene came over, her blond hair anchored at the back of her head in a sort of half ponytail that bounced as she walked. Her wide mouth was stretched in a welcoming smile. She handed them each a menu, congratulated Angie on her marriage to Brett and asked, "Iced tea?"

"Sounds good," said Angie.

Glory was nodding. "Make that two." Then she scowled. "Wait. Scratch that. Just one." She held up the water glass Charlene had already set in front of her. "I'll have plain water. Nursing. It's not for sissies."

Charlene laughed and trotted off.

Angie unrolled the paper napkin from around her flatware. "Where's Johnny?"

"At home. Mamma's watching him—and did you hear?" Glory glanced around to make sure no one was listening. She leaned close and whispered, "Sissy came back." Sissy Cooper was Charlene's baby sister. She'd been sent off to live with relatives when their parents went over the cliff. "Gone Goth. Safety pins in her nose, black lipstick, spiky purple hair. And this is the good part…" Glory paused for effect before delivering the bombshell in a whisper low enough that Angie barely heard it. "Brand gave her a job."

Charlene and Brand Bravo had been high school sweethearts. But they'd had a falling out of some sort. A serious one. The rift had never been mended. Nowadays, they'd walk across the street to avoid running into each other—which made Brand's hiring Sissy pretty surprising.

Glory went on, "Sissy is now Brand's receptionist and clerk. Can't you just see her, safety pins sticking out everywhere, filing a brief, or whatever it is they do in a lawyer's office? She started this morning."

Angie made a big show of looking at her watch. "And now it's almost noon, so everyone in town has heard all about it."

Glory giggled. "Got that right. And I have to tell you, it's a relief every once in a while to have folks talking about somebody other than me."

Charlene reappeared with Angie's iced tea. "The usual for both of you?"

"Thanks," said Angie.

"Yeah," said Glory. Charlene waltzed off. Glory grinned. "And Sissy's return isn't all folks are talkin' about. There's also you." She raised her water glass in a toast.

Angie sipped her tea and asked, all innocence, "What do you mean, me?"

"Well, you and the wonderful, one-and-only Dr. Brett. It's a big deal around town—and I mean in a *good* way. You know. Romantic, all that. You two running off to Reno…" Glory lowered her voice again. "And everyone knows you've been in that house by the river all weekend—with the blinds closed."

Angie thought of those few crucial moments before they'd shut the blinds and hoped her face wasn't as red as it felt. She said, deadpan, "We had a tough week, workwise. We were very, very tired."

"Sleeping. Ha. Right." Glory reached across and brushed her shoulder with a fond hand. "You look…terrific, you know that?"

"Er, I do?"

"Oh, yeah. All soft and glowing."

Angie couldn't hide her smile anymore. She felt it bloom wide. "Well. I guess that's because I'm happy." She picked up her tea again.

Glory said, "I always wondered when you and Brett would finally get together."

Angie set down her glass without drinking from it. "So did everyone else in town, apparently—except Brett and me, I mean."

"Well, at least you figured it out at last. You've been in love with that guy since forever. And don't give me that huffy look. Brett's always been the only one for you."

"You think so?"

"I know so."

Angie leaned really close to her sister and whispered, "Then what about Jody?"

Glory snapped her fingers. "Nothin', that's what. A way to work through your frustrations at waiting so long to come on home and get what you really want."

Why argue? Angie thought. No, she wasn't in love with Brett. She never had been. But things really had worked out just great and that was what mattered.

"And you know what?" Glory fluttered her eyelashes as she paused for effect. "I do believe that's a hickey on the side of your neck."

Angie resisted the urge to put her hand over the spot. She'd covered it with makeup—she thought.

Glory laughed. "Oh, don't worry. It's not that noticeable—unless someone's lookin' for it."

Angie tried a stern expression. "And now, little sister. We need to talk about *you.*"

"Admit it. You're nuts for the guy."

Angie knew she was busted. "Okay. The truth is, it's incredible...."

"It?"

Angie mouthed the letters S-E-X. "This morning, at the clinic, I had to constantly remind myself to keep my mind on my job and not on my husband's totally hot body."

"This is a problem?"

"Well, he *is* a doctor. And I'm a nurse. People count

on us to be paying attention when we're giving them injections and performing minor surgeries. The last thing we need is to be distracting each other on the job."

Glory wasn't especially sympathetic. "Buck up. You'll get used to all this happiness, just wait and see."

Their sandwiches came, a matched pair of BLTs on whole wheat, each with a beautiful mound of French fries on the side. As they shoveled the food in, Glory finally opened up and vented a little.

The family was driving her crazy. She had to get out—and she was taking Johnny and moving back to Chastity's that afternoon. "Mom's freaking out about it. She wants me and Johnny to stay at home—unless I agree to marry Bowie. Then it would be fine with her if I left, as long as I was moving in with him."

"But you're not."

"Nope. That's just asking for trouble, to get myself hooked up to a guy as messed up as Bowie."

"But you still love him."

"Hey, what can I tell you? It's like a chronic disease, my love for that guy. Somehow, I've got to learn to live with my affliction."

"Can I help, today, with your move to the Sierra Star?"

"Nope. Got it handled. Chastity's got that old pickup and Brand said he'd pitch in. Alyosha's bringing his pickup, too." Alyosha Panopopoulis was Chastity's boyfriend. They'd been going out since before Christmas. From what Angie had heard, Alyosha was the second man, ever, in Chastity's life—the first, of course, being her rarely there, now-dead, psycho-dog husband Blake. "I've got everything packed," Glory assured her. "And I'm only moving down the street, anyway."

"What else can I do to help? Anything. Just name it."

Glory pointed at her plate. "This. Buy me lunch now and then. Listen to me rant."

"Okay, then. Once a week. Monday at eleven-thirty, right here in this booth. Shake on it." She held out her hand.

Glory took it and they shook to seal the deal.

Angie's first week as Mrs. Brett Bravo flew by in a haze of hard work—and great sex. She did manage to get down to Grass Valley on Wednesday to see her gynecologist and get a new diaphragm, but other than that, she and Brett were together constantly.

Oh, she could not get enough of that man.

Brett seemed to feel the same way about her. They'd lock the clinic doors at five and race home, where they'd run around the great room yanking all the blinds down and then fall on each other like a couple of sex-starved teenagers.

By Friday night, as they lay in bed, cuddled up close, appeased for the moment, they agreed that they really needed to get out of the house, to do something in their spare time that included clothing and contact with the outside world.

"Oh, I suppose we should," murmured Angie, and

snuggled in with a sigh, thinking that it didn't get any better than this: Brett's big arms around her, her head pillowed on his hard chest, listening to the steady beat of his heart.

He stroked her hair, idly ran his hand down her back, setting off a chain of lovely warm shivers in the wake of that gentle touch. "Tomorrow's the spring dance…" In the Flat, there were usually four community-run dances a year, one for each season, held upstairs in the town hall next door to the firehouse. His voice rumbled beneath her ear as he added, "We could grab a couple of steaks at the Nugget first. What do you say?"

"Fine with me," she whispered, sliding her hand down under the blankets and wrapping her fingers around him, so warm and innocent and soft—at first. She squeezed, gently. His response was immediate: a delicious thickening as he hardened….

He made a low sound—part growl, part groan. "You're going to kill me, you know that."

"Oh, but what a sweet way to go…"

Brett anticipated an intimate dinner at the Nugget with his wife. But when they got there the next evening, Brett's mother and her boyfriend, Alyosha, were sitting in "their" booth.

"Hey." Nadine shrugged. "If I'd a known you two were coming, I'd a stuck a reserved sign on it. How's married life treating you?"

"Wonderful." Angie replied.

Brett liked the warm, excited way she said that. He glanced over to meet her eyes. Heat arced between them. He watched her swallow.

He knew what she was thinking. He was thinking it, too. It was good to be out together, but nowhere near as good as being home, where they could do whatever came naturally—and then do it again.

And Nadine was still prattling away. "Well, nothin' like mad love, I always say." Irritation flashed through him. *Mad love.* Hardly. Not him and Angie. They were smarter than that. "You mind a table instead of a booth this time?"

Brett didn't mind in the least. He didn't care where they sat—or what they ate. It was ironic, really. He'd been the one who suggested they ought to go out—and already he wanted to grab his bride, throw her over his shoulder and head for home, where he would waste no time getting her out of the sexy short skirt she was wearing and back into bed. He put a hand at the small of her back—so she would look at him again and also for the simple, stunning pleasure that touching her always brought.

"You mind?" he asked. She shook her head. He told Nadine, "A table's fine."

But by then Alyosha was sliding out of his side of the booth and in next to Chastity. "Come on, you two." He waved them on. "You join us. We have plenty of room."

So they sat with his mother and her date. Brett would have preferred it to be just the two of them—but at least, this way, he and Angie ended up side-by-side. Now and then, just in passing, they would touch. She would brush her arm against his, or her thigh would press his as she shifted those long legs of hers.

His nerves hummed with the constant awareness of her—the scent of her, the way the light made her brown hair shine, those gorgeous dimples that curved along her soft cheeks each time she smiled. He wanted to stick out his tongue and lick them, lick *her.* Every inch of her.

But they were out in public, so he had to behave himself. And in spite of the torment of having to wait till they got home to make love with her, it was good, he thought. Real good. Sitting in that booth with his wife at his side; seeing Ma so happy, at last, with a man.

Alyosha was a widower, retired. He worked as a handyman to supplement his reduced income. He had a kind heart and a level head and he laughed often and easily. Brett was glad that at last Ma had found a guy like this, after all that his bad dad had put her through.

After the meal, they walked across the street to the dance together, the four of them. By then, it was full dark, a cool spring night with the stars thick overhead. Golden light poured out the open double doors of the town hall, along with the music from a local five-piece band.

Sidney Potter was selling tickets, her broken leg stuck out to the side and her crutches propped within reach against the nearby wall. She took their money and congratulated Brett and Angie on their newlywed status.

"How's that leg feeling?" he asked as she passed him two tickets.

Sidney winked at him. "Until I try to stand up, I hardly know it's broken."

They went on upstairs, gave their tickets at the door and entered the rustic ballroom, which was paneled— walls, ceiling and floor—like the Nugget, in knotty-pine. Built-in pine benches lined three of the walls. Open double doors on the street side let in the cool night air and led to a wide balcony that overlooked Main. At the far end of the room, opposite the entry doors, the Salty Dog Band blared out "Tequila Sunrise" up on the simple platform stage.

The band wasn't that great, but at least it was a ballad. That meant he had an excuse to take Angie in his arms. He pulled her to him and they two-stepped out onto the floor. A good dancer, she followed him effortlessly.

Years ago, when they were in high school, he used to dance with her all the time. After all, they were pals and he knew she liked to dance. If he noticed her sitting on the sidelines, he would always step up and offer to be her partner so she could get out on the floor. Then, when the song was over, he would let her go with a smile and an easy, "See you later, Angie."

Back then, he realized now, he'd been a damn fool who'd had no idea what he was missing.

She let out a low, throaty laugh, the sound cascading through him, arousing him the way everything else about her aroused him. She teased, "Bet I know what you're thinkin'."

"Hit me with it."

"The old days. You and me, dancing, right here in the old knotty-pine ballroom, same as now—and yet so completely different."

That was another incredible thing about her: the way she could read him, the way she so instinctively got what was going on inside him. "Okay, admit it. You've got psychic powers."

She dimpled at him. "Well, the truth is, I just happened to be thinking the same thing."

He wanted to kiss her, right there on the dance floor. But if he kissed her, he wasn't sure he'd be able to stop. So he settled for pulling her just a fraction closer. He felt her warm breath against his neck. And her light, cool, tempting touch: one hand in his, the other on his shoulder. And he *was* holding her, guiding her, with his palm at her lower back.

Dancing wasn't so bad. Not as good as making love with her—but then, nothing was as good as that.

He kept her in his arms for the next three dances. And then Anthony cut in, so he had to let her go. After that there were three fast ones. Each dance, Brett would start toward her, but some other guy would get to her first. It was kind of funny, really, how he'd miss out every time. Not that it was any big deal. During the fast dances, the partners hardly touched, anyway. The guys who got to her first didn't even have their arms around her.

When the next slow one came, Brett was too late again. Brand stepped up to Angie before he could reach her. So he danced with Dani, all the while acutely conscious that Angie was dancing with someone else— even though that someone else was his own brother.

Dani gazed up at him, dewy-eyed and sighing. "It's so beautiful. I mean, after all this time, I was beginning to wonder if you and Angie would ever get together. But look at you. Married at last and totally in love…"

He almost blurted out in a growl, *You don't get it. It's not like that.*

Somehow he bit off the sharp words before they escaped him. And he wondered at his own over-the-top reaction. Why should an innocent remark from Dani bother him so much?

He *did* love Angie.

Just not in the way everyone seemed to think.

He loved Angie, but he wasn't *in love* with Angie. And she wasn't in love with him. That was the beauty of what they had. They were best friends and they were partners—at work and at home. And there was the sex thing, which continued to flat-out astonish him, it was so good.

But they weren't *in love.*

And did Dani need to know all that?

Hardly.

He composed his expression into an easy smile. "Yeah. She's really something. I'm a lucky man."

* * *

After Brett danced with Dani, a ghoulish little thing in a short black skirt with spiked maroon hair, safety pins all over her face, combat boots and one of those lace-up leather bustier things strutted up to him. "Hey, Brett Bravo. I know you."

He peered at her more closely. "Sissy? Sissy Cooper?" Last time he'd seen Sissy, she'd been eight or nine, a sweet, skinny little thing with big blue eyes. He only recognized her now because he'd heard she was in town again—and that she liked to wear safety pins for jewelry.

"You got it." She grinned, black-painted lips tipping up at the corners, the safety pin stuck in her left eyebrow glittering. "I'm back in town and workin' for your brother."

"So I heard."

"How 'bout a dance?"

What could he say? It was another slow one. He took her lightly in his arms and led her out on the floor.

Immediately he wished he'd figured out a way to turn her down gently and sit this one out. Through the whole dance, she kept trying to get in closer to him. Once, she even pretended to trip so she could plaster her grown-up little body all over the front of him. She smelled of bargain-brand cigarettes. And when she looked up at him, he wondered what she was on. Her blue eyes were black holes, the irises swallowed by the dilated pupils.

Sissy, evidently, had changed a lot in the past decade or so—and not for the better. Brett wondered that his brother had hired her to work for him.

But then again, maybe Brand was only to trying to make up for whatever had gone so wrong between him and Sissy's big sister, Charlene, all those years ago. Brett could understand how Brand might want make amends, to help Sissy out a little, so he and Charlene could let bygones be bygones.

Back in the day, Brand had been crazy-wild for Charlene….

Not a moment too soon for Brett, the dance with Sissy came to an end. He took her by her tiny cinched-in waist and set her firmly away from him. "Sissy, you take care now."

He turned and left her, fast, on the creepy off chance that she might throw herself at him again and demand the next dance, too.

He didn't want to dance with Charlene Cooper's strange little sister. He wanted to dance with his wife, damn it. And he'd lost sight of Angie while trying to keep the scary new Sissy from crawling all over him.

The hall was pretty full by then, the floor packed with whirling couples. Folks who weren't dancing were perched on the built-in benches along the walls, or hanging around the refreshment tables up by the stage. Brett circled the room, waving at friends and neighbors as he passed them, weaving his way through the crush.

He found his brothers not far from the doors to the

balcony. Bowie was braced against a wall, head down, sagging as if someone had hung him out to dry. Brand was right beside him, saying something in his ear.

Brett called to them and Brand glanced over. Bowie slowly lifted his head. Those drooping eyes of his said it all: hammered. Again.

Well, at least Glory had shown the good sense to stay home tonight. Without Glory here to shout at, Bowie was a lot less likely act like an ass. He'd probably just drink until he fell over. After that, if he was lucky, some kind soul would make sure he got home and into bed.

Pitiful. Sick. The guy was out of control and in serious need of an intervention. Brett made a mental note to talk to Ma about that.

"Seen Angie?" Brett shouted, in hopes they could hear him over the pounding bass guitar.

Brand shook his head. Bowie rolled those bloodshot eyes and drooped against the wall again.

So okay, Brett thought, he'd give the balcony a try. She wasn't out there. He went back inside.

As he stepped in through the open doors, he spotted her—up by the stage with some guy he'd never seen before. Momentarily, the press of dancing couples blocked the two from his sight, and then, as the dancers moved on, revealed them again.

Angie didn't look happy. She was frowning and shaking her head.

The guy beside her wore an open flannel shirt, sagging khakis and a shifty expression. Brett's first angry thought was, *Jody? Could* this be the bastard who'd hurt her so bad?

But no. Angie had said Jody was a big guy, a biker type. This guy was maybe five-eight and scrawny. Plus, Angie seemed more annoyed than anything. From what she'd told Brett, she might have any number of highly emotional reactions if she ran into Jody again.

But mere annoyance? No way.

Brett relaxed a little.

The guy said something. Angie kept shaking her head. More couples danced by. When they passed, the skinny guy had Angie by the arm.

At the sight of that scrawny creep's hand on his wife, something dark and dangerous slammed through Brett. Swearing under his breath, dodging dancing couples as he went, he advanced on them.

Angie yanked free. Her lips moved. Brett couldn't hear the words, but he thought she said, "Please don't." She turned to walk away.

The guy wouldn't give up. He trotted along behind her, wrinkled shirttail flying, trying to grab her again.

Brett kept moving their way, the blood spurting hot and fast through his veins. He wanted to hit something—specifically, the S.O.B. in the flannel shirt who was harassing his wife.

She whirled on the guy, and that time she got right in his face. Whatever she said, it did the job. She held up her ring finger and shook it at him. The guy blinked, stepped back—and then turned and slunk off, looking like nothing so much as a mangy, whupped dog.

Brett froze in midstride twenty feet from his wife and let the hot flood of protective rage inside him fade down to something less urgent—but no less disturbing.

He'd been out of control. Flat-out, ugly, bust-your-face-in furious. If Angie hadn't gotten rid of that idiot before Brett got to him, Brett would have punched the fool's lights out, possibly even started a regular Bravo-style brawl, right here in the town hall.

He would have popped that guy a good one—and not thought twice about it.

What the hell was the matter with him?

Angie could handle a guy like that with her eyes closed and one hand tied behind her back. She *had* handled him, efficiently and with a minimum of fuss. And even if it *had* come down differently, even if it had been necessary for Brett to step in and help her out, there was no damn sense in him acting like his crazy, dead dad or his wild-man baby brother.

Brett had always prided himself on how he never descended to testosterone-driven crap like that.

Brett was a reasonable man.

He wasn't the caveman type.

Or at least, he'd never been before. Until tonight. Over Angie.

She turned and saw him, her sweet face lighting up, soft mouth lifting in that unforgettable dimpled smile. Something hot and wild rose within him. Something every bit as dangerous as his raging fury of a moment before.

It hit him. Right there on the dance floor. The hard truth came at him swift, sure and shattering as a wrecking ball.

He was wild for Angie. *Crazy* for Angie…

All he'd wanted was a happy, settled, *normal* life. And here he was, barely married a week, a marriage that was supposed to be sane and mutually supportive and completely free of all the craziness that came with romance and passionate love…

Married a week…and he had gone and fallen, head-over-heels, for his wife.

How could this have happened?

And what in hell was he going to do about it?

He had no answer to either question.

She held out her hand to him. He took it, felt the heat, the dangerous power of his desire for her, as it radiated through him. A slow song started up.

He pulled her into his arms. She rested her head on his shoulder.

They danced into the center of the crowd. Only then did he whisper, "Who was that skinny guy?"

She sighed. "Joel, I think he said his name was. From Modesto—and I do hope he goes back there soon. I danced with him once and then he wouldn't leave me alone. I had to wave my wedding ring in his face to finally get rid of him."

"I saw that." Brett held her closer, breathing in the scent that belonged only to her. "Good job."

"I felt a little sorry for him. I mean, he did seem kind of lonely…"

"Stay the hell away from him." He tried to make it sound teasing—but it wasn't.

She nodded against his shoulder. "Don't worry. I'm having nothin' to do with him—and I saw you with Sissy. That girl was on you like chrome on a trailer hitch. Brett, it's so sad. I mean, she's hardly more than a kid…."

"Yeah, well. She's not the same little Sissy we all used to know."

"Stay the hell away from her." She imitated his tone of a moment before.

"Not a problem. She's way too young for me. And I've never been partial to that whole safety-pin thing—and, most of all…"

She lifted her head and pressed her lips to his neck. Heat sizzled through him. She whispered, "Here comes the good part…."

He nuzzled the tender shape of her ear. "I could never look twice at her. Or at any other woman. Because none of them is you."

Chapter Seven

Angie didn't really understand how it happened—or even what, exactly, *had* happened. But after the spring dance, things weren't the same between her and Brett.

Something was…missing. She just couldn't quite put her finger on what.

Then again, maybe it was only her imagination. After all, he still reached for her with the same urgency and hunger as he had the first time they made love. When he kissed her, when he touched her, when he moved so slow and sweet inside her…her doubts blew away. When he loved her, her fears would ease. That vague sense of loss would leave her. She would know then that nothing was wrong, that her life had never been so right.

Then again…

But no.

She was sure it was nothing. They had a wonderful life together and everything was fine.

The late-spring days passed, each one a little longer and warmer than the one before it.

Brett said that Chastity had had a long talk with Bowie. The talk must have done some good; miracle of miracles, Bowie actually seemed to be straightening up. He cut the drinking way back and the second week in June, he got a job—tending bar at the St. Thomas, of all things.

The following Monday, during their weekly lunch date at the diner, Angie heard from Glory that folks in town were taking bets on how long Bowie would last, both on the job and also until he got smashed and got up to his old tricks again.

"That's so cruel," Angie told Brett at home over dinner that night. "The poor guy's doing his best to make a change in his life and everybody in town is betting on when he's going to blow it."

Brett only shrugged. "What's that old saying? Life's hard. Then you die." He turned his attention back to his plate.

Several seconds ticked by. Angie thought how the silence between them didn't feel as comfortable as it had in the past.

But that was silly.

Wasn't it?

And on second thought, maybe it wasn't the quality

of the silence so much, as it was how they didn't *talk* the way they did at first.

She tried again. "Still, though. Sometimes I think Bowie's just a guy who does what everyone expects of him—which is to mess up, over and over again."

Brett sent her a cool and distant glance. "It's no one's fault but his own that Bowie's screwed things up for himself."

"I didn't say it was anyone's fault, I just said, it seems to me that people only make things worse by *betting* on how and when the poor guy's going to fail."

"How many times have we been through this?"

She truly didn't get his attitude. What had she said? She wanted to snap at him, to tell him to stop being a condescending jerk, but she knew that wouldn't help. With effort, she kept her tone level and reasonable. "You mean, how many times have we talked about how everybody's betting that Bowie will fail? This is the first, as far as I recall."

"I don't mean about Bowie, specifically. I mean about the Flat. I mean about how, in a small town like ours, you've got to learn to take the good with the bad."

"Well, I understand that. I do. I'm just saying—"

"I know what you're saying. And it doesn't matter."

She stiffened. "It doesn't matter what I say?"

"Yes, it *does* matter what you say," he replied with a patronizing kind of patience that set her teeth on edge. "It *doesn't* matter that people are thoughtless and even downright cruel."

"I don't agree. People give what they get. If all they get is cruelty, well, how else can you expect them to behave in return?"

"Angie, the point is, either a man gets on with it and gets his life in order, or he doesn't. If he blows it all to hell, it's his fault and his alone."

"Whew." She set down her fork. "That's harsh."

"It's called reality. We all have to live with it."

"Maybe so. But I'm not going to just sit by and say nothing. Anybody starts running Bowie down when I'm around, predicting how he'll screw up, they're going to get an earful from me."

"Go ahead. Tell them how wrong they are."

"I intend to."

"It's pointless. But go right ahead."

She stared at him across the table, thinking how grim he looked, how lately he seemed to be changing. And not for the better.

He frowned back at her. "What?" She swallowed, suddenly nervous, not knowing quite how to say it. Until he prodded again, "What?"

"Well, is there something…wrong? Something I'm doing that's bothering you? Something about me you really don't like?"

"No," he said. "To all three questions."

She waited for him to ask why. When he didn't, she told him anyway. "You're just….different. I don't know. As if something's eating at you. Are you sure there's nothing?"

His gaze slid away. When it swung back to meet

hers, his eyes had softened. He even reached across the table and laid his hand over hers. "Sorry." His thumb brushed the notch between her thumb and forefinger, sliding underneath until he was rubbing her palm.

All at once she was breathless, her blood somehow thicker, her pulse more insistent as it pushed through her veins. "Not fair," she accused on a torn breath.

His thumb traced a secret pattern in the hidden heart of her palm. "We should eat dinner naked."

She laughed then, low and huskily, and told herself her fears were totally groundless. There was nothing wrong between them. They disagreed now and then, on various issues. So what? Disagreement was healthy. Perfectly normal.

And what were they talking about, anyway?

Oh, yeah. She repeated in a musing tone, "Eating dinner naked…"

Those dark eyes of his sparkled with naughty promises of future delights. "What do you think?"

"Uh-uh."

"Why not?"

"Too distracting. We'd never eat. We'd waste away to nothing."

"Aren't you the one who's always saying 'what a way to go'?"

"Yeah, but, well, over time, we'd just get used to it— to being naked at the table. It would get so it wasn't distracting at all."

He wore a puzzled frown. "And that would be bad?"

"No. It would be sad. Very sad." Reluctantly she pulled her hand out from under his and back to her side of the table. "Now, eat your pork chop."

"And then what?"

"Eat your peas, too. And your potato."

"Yes, Mother. And then?"

She slipped off her sandal and reached out with her foot, catching his cuff with her toe, wiggling that toe upward, so she could rub his hard, hairy leg with it. "Whatever you want."

His plate was clean in record time.

Angie's vague uneasiness about her relationship with Brett never completely went away.

He did seem…different. Distracted, or something. Like he had a secret he wouldn't—or couldn't—share. They really *didn't* talk the way they used to, did they? And sometimes she'd find him watching her and she'd wonder what in the world he might be thinking.

She'd ask him.

And he'd say something teasing. "I'm thinking how gorgeous you are…."

Or something evasive. "Nothing. Not a damn thing. My mind's a total blank."

Never once did he admit that something was going on with him. So she stopped asking. She didn't want to be a nag.

Friday night, four nights after they disagreed over Bowie, they went out to the Nugget after work.

They'd just settled into their booth when the door to the street opened.

And in walked Joel whatever-his-last-name-was, the skinny guy from Modesto who'd given Angie grief at the spring dance. He spotted Angie and he waved. Angie thought he looked kind of sheepish, kind of sorry for how he'd behaved before, and he had on a clean shirt, buttoned this time, even tucked in. She almost waved back, just to signal she was willing to let bygones be bygones.

But on second thought, no. She didn't know him. He might be the type to interpret her waving at him as an invitation to start hassling her all over again.

Brett saw her glance toward the door. He turned to follow the direction of her gaze. "Be right back." His voice was calm.

Too calm. An absolute stillness seemed to emanate from him, a stillness with a promise of swift violence to come.

Brett about to pick a fight?

Uh-uh. Fighting wasn't his style. Bowie picked fights. And Buck used to, in the old days. Brand might even mix it up now and then, with enough provocation.

But not Brett. Brett was the *reasonable* one. He never lost his temper. His weapons of choice were his clear head and quick wit.

Still, dread stole through Angie. "Brett…" She reached to stop him, but he was already up out of the booth and striding toward Joel.

Angie clapped a hand over her mouth to keep herself

from screeching frantically, *"Brett! Don't!"* She watched her husband march right up to the poor guy—and whisper in his ear.

That was it. A whisper. And a brief one, at that.

Joel stiffened and staggered back, though Brett hadn't so much as touched him. And then he pivoted on his heel, flung the door wide and got the heck out of there.

Nadine, strolling over with a menu in her hand, grumbled, "What's going on, Brett? You scaring my customers away?"

"Not me. Looks like the guy suddenly decided he had a pressing appointment."

With a shrug, Nadine dropped the menu in the stand by the door and went to pick up an order. Brett rejoined Angie in the booth.

She stared at him, wide-eyed.

He growled, "What?"

She gulped. "Um. Nothing…" Who was this person sitting across from her? Surely not the levelheaded, easygoing man she had married. She grabbed one of the menus Nadine had left on the table and studied it for all she was worth.

"Angie…"

She shifted behind her menu, but she didn't put it down. "Hmm?"

"Look at me." Why was that so hard to do? She made herself lower the menu a little and peered cautiously over the top of it. His gaze locked on hers. "Put the menu down."

"Fine." She set it back on top of the other one, gulped again, and admitted, "I thought you were going to bust him a good one."

"But I didn't."

"What awful thing did you say to him?"

"'Get lost.'"

"That's all?"

"That's all."

"You really scared him."

"I intended to scare him."

"You, um, scared me, too. You just…" She didn't know how to go on. And there seemed no real point in going on. It all led back to the strange changes in him lately, the changes he flatly denied every time she dared to try to talk about them.

He didn't encourage her to continue, to finish what she'd started to say. He only muttered, "I'm sorry I scared you."

And she said, "It's okay," though it wasn't. Not really. Lately, things between them seemed less and less okay. She couldn't figure out why. And he wasn't even willing to talk about it. "We should order," she said.

He caught Nadine's eye and signaled her over. They ordered. The food came. They ate.

Later, they went home and made beautiful love together.

And late in the night, Angie lay wide awake beside her sleeping husband and tried to tell herself that things between them weren't slowly going terribly wrong.

She really needed to talk to somebody about all this. Since Brett *wouldn't* talk to her, she'd have to find someone else she could trust to confide in....

Chapter Eight

Glory set down her sandwich and leaned close. "Fear of intimacy," she said in an ominous tone. When Angie frowned at her, Glory elaborated, keeping her voice low so no one else would hear. "I read this long article about men who are afraid to get close. In *American Woman* magazine."

"You think Brett's afraid of…getting close to me?"

"Oh, yeah." Glory pulled a loose piece of bacon out of the side of her sandwich and popped it into her mouth. She chewed, thoughtfully. "Deep down, they're all—all of Chastity's sons—afraid of trusting, of letting a woman get too close. So far, only Buck's gotten over it. When I think of how openly and honestly he loves B.J., it can almost give me hope for Bowie and me." She dredged a French fry in ketchup and thoughtfully nibbled the end of it. "But then I think, uh-uh. Bowie's too scared to get down and get equal with me. He always thinks he has to boss me around. That's *his* way of keeping me at arm's distance, emotionally speaking. And Brett and Brand, well, they have different ways of showing it, but they never really let anybody get close, either."

Angie thought of her first days on the job at the clinic, of the initial weeks of their marriage, of how she and Brett would sit and talk for hours on end back then, how open and free it had all seemed.

"But Glory, Brett *did* let me get close. At first. It's only lately that he's gotten so distant, that I've started to feel like I don't really even know him."

Glory pointed with her red-tipped French fry. "See? That's the fear kicking in."

"But…why? What does he have to be afraid of?"

"Well, I don't know. It's not like I'm a shrink or anything. Maybe he just doesn't know…how to *be* a husband."

Angie blew out an impatient breath. "But I told you. He was doing great. At the beginning…"

"Like I said, then the fear kicked in."

"But—"

Glory put up a hand. "Think about this. It's not like any of those four boys ever had any example of the way it's supposed to work between a man and a woman. I mean, they hardly knew their father. Bowie never knew Blake at all. He was long gone before Bowie was even born. And when the other three were really little, the way Chastity tells it, Blake would show up for a week or two, and then vanish for months, a year, even longer. For the boys, it was the same as not even having a dad. Their dad was a stranger to them, a scary guy they didn't know, a dangerous guy who would show up now and then and sleep in their mother's room.

"And, Chastity…well, I love her. We all love her. But she was a different person then. She's changed a lot—for the better—over the years. Mostly, when the boys were growing up, she was an overworked single mom, running her business and putting all her spare energy into dreaming about Blake coming back to her. She loved the boys, but she wasn't giving them the firm hand and the attention they needed." Glory chomped another piece of bacon. "And I'm not talking out of turn. Chastity's the first one to admit she could have done a better job as a mom."

"So…their father was never there. And Chastity didn't pay enough attention to them. And that makes them afraid to get close to a woman they care about?"

"Yeah. It's like…they never learned *how*—not to mention they're afraid of loving someone so much, they can't live without her. They're afraid they could end up like Chastity, left behind with a broken heart."

Angie slumped back against the tufted red vinyl of the booth. "I don't know. I don't think I buy it…" She took the sprig of parsley from the side of her plate and twirled it slowly by the stem.

Glory picked up her sandwich again. "Well. It's just a thought, you know—and stop playing with your food. Eat."

"Okay, okay." Angie tossed the parsley back on the plate and ate a French fry. "Sometimes, I wonder if it's what Aunt Stella said." When Glory sent her a questioning glance, she explained, "You know the old saying about marrying in haste—and repenting at leisure?"

Glory snorted. "Aunt Stella said that after you eloped with Brett?"

"Well, sort of. She said a marriage in haste isn't a marriage at all."

Glory groaned. "Come on. You know you're in trouble if you start taking Aunt Stella too seriously. She should have gotten married herself, had some kids …committed a few sins of her own, for cryin' out loud, given herself something to atone for. Or maybe even become a nun. Aunt Stella might have actually been happy as a nun. Instead, she stayed single and moved in with Mamma and she's got way too much free time on her hands—free time that she uses to tell everyone else how to live."

"But, Brett and me, we *did* rush into it…."

"Oh, come on. You said it yourself. You've known the guy all your life. It's not like he's some stranger— and you can have your marriage blessed by Father Delahunty, if that's what's really bothering you."

"I know. We will. But first, I'd like to figure out what's bothering my *husband*."

"Fear of intimacy," Glory said, looking much too smug for a woman who was in love with Bowie Bravo. "Think about it."

Charlene came over and refilled Angie's iced tea.

When she left, Glory spoke out of the side of her mouth. "Wait'll you hear what I heard…juicy. Very juicy."

Angie pulled her shoulders back. "Gossip, you mean?"

"That's right."

"After what you told me last week, about everyone betting on how soon Bowie's going to blow it, I've been thinking I don't approve of gossip all that much."

Glory nibbled yet another French fry. Slowly. "Well. Okay, then. If you don't wanna know…"

Angie held on to her nobility for maybe three seconds. "Tell me."

"You're sure? I mean, if you don't *approve*…"

"Oh, cut it out and tell me."

Glory giggled, bent close again and whispered, "It's Sissy. She's split town. Evidently she left some time in the middle of the night last night. Charlene told me that when she got up this morning, Sissy was gone and so were all her things."

Angie sent a glance Charlene's way. Sissy's big sister was over behind the counter, refilling coffee cups, her wide mouth a grim line. "I thought Charlene seemed a little downhearted today."

"And Sissy taking off out of nowhere isn't all of it."

"Oh, God. What else?"

"Last night, somebody let themselves into Brand's office, tore the place up, and took off with the petty cash drawer."

"And they think it was Sissy?"

"It wasn't a break-in. Someone let themselves in. Sissy had a key, so it kinda looks she did it."

"Poor Charlene," said Angie.

"Poor Brand," said Glory. "All he did was try to help out."

Angie realized she'd been so busy talking about her own problems, she hadn't even asked Glory how things were going in *her* life. "How's my new nephew?"

Glory's eyes got softer and the Dellazola dimples appeared in her cheeks. "He's a good baby, the best thing that ever happened to me."

"Things still working out for you over at Chastity's?"

"Mm-hmm. We take turns looking after Johnny. It works out real well. She's a terrific Grandma, she really is. And also a great person to have as a friend."

Angie had to ask. "And…you and Bowie?"

Glory shook her head. "There *is* no me and Bowie, not anymore. I doubt there ever will be again."

"But he's doing better, right?"

"So I hear. And one thing I'll say for him lately, since Chastity had that long talk with him, he's been sober when he shows up at the B and B. He's still got that bad attitude, but he doesn't order me to marry him.

He asks in a sulky kind of way. I tell him no. And then he leaves."

Angie reached across the table and stroked a hand down her sister's silky hair. "I'm sorry, Glory...."

Glory shrugged. "I'm telling you. Fear of intimacy. The Bravo boys have got it bad."

That evening, Brett had two emergency calls back-to-back. For the second one, he had to get the patient to the hospital in Grass Valley, run some tests and wait for the results before he could set a course of treatment.

Angie fixed dinner for two and put Brett's in the fridge for him to heat up later. She sat down and ate alone and then cleaned up the kitchen a little.

She was just settling in front of the TV in the great room, thinking she'd watch a movie or something, take her mind off her vague, persistent worries that things weren't right with Brett, when the phone rang.

Angie answered and her aunt Stella said, "It's us." Meaning Angie's mom was on the line, too. They liked to get on the phone together, her mom and her aunt, one on the kitchen extension and one in the living room. "Are we interrupting your dinner?"

"No. It's fine. I already ate."

"How's Dr. Brett?" asked her mother.

Angie explained that he was with a patient, in Grass Valley.

"A wonderful man," declared Aunt Stella. "Kind,

CHRISTINE RIMMER 137

thoughtful and good—and you haven't been to see Father Delahunty."

Angie had known that was coming. "No. But I will."

Stella chided, "We haven't seen you at mass recently…."

Since she hadn't married in the Church, Angie wasn't supposed to take communion, and if she didn't take communion she knew her aunt would just *have* to give her a hard time about it. Why even go?

"Don't start in on me. Please?"

The line was quiet for ten full seconds. Angie could just see her mother and her aunt, biting their tongues in unison on their separate extensions.

Finally, in a tone of utmost dignity, Stella announced, "Old Tony turns ninety next week." Great-Grandpa Tony had been born on the Fourth of July, a fact that pleased him no end, as he considered himself a true patriot. The family always had a big party on the Fourth, to celebrate both the holiday and Old Tony's birthday.

Angie asked, "So what's the plan?"

"Well," said her mother, her voice dripping with significance. "We thought a barbecue. Maybe down by the river…"

Angie took the hint. "We could have it here." With the river and that nice beach just down the trail across the road, the house she shared with Brett was a perfect location for a summer barbecue.

She found herself wondering, Would Brett mind?

It made her kind of sad that the thought even

occurred to her. In the first days of her marriage, the question would never have come up. She would have known without even having to think about it that Brett would be pleased to host a big family party.

Nowadays, though…

She didn't have a clue how Brett felt about things.

"Oh, Angie…" gushed her mother. "I knew you'd say that. We wanted it to be extra special for Old Tony's ninetieth. We are going to have ourselves a beautiful party."

"The best ever," declared Aunt Stella.

And then they were off and running, talking over each other, making their plans, giving each other orders, discussing how they'd set up the picnic tables on the deck, who should bring what and how early in the day they'd need to take over Angie's kitchen. Angie listened and made agreeable noises and hoped that Brett wouldn't mind.

Brett *didn't* mind. Not in the least. When she asked him that night, he told her he thought it was a great idea.

Which she should have known, really.

But she'd doubted, because they just didn't communicate the way they used to.

"Maybe we could invite Ma, too," he suggested. They were lying in bed by then with the lights out. "I mean, if you think that would be okay with your family…"

"Are you kidding? The more the merrier as far as they're concerned. And how about Brand? Maybe he'd like to come."

"I'll ask him."

"Good." She thought of Bowie. They really should ask him, too, but she hesitated to mention him. You never knew what kind of stunt Bowie might pull.

Brett's teeth flashed white through the darkness as he grinned at her. She grinned back and at that moment, it was just like it used to be, easy and clear between them, both of them on the same wavelength.

"Bowie," they said in unison.

She asked, "What do you think?"

"Well, he *has* been behaving himself lately. He's still got his job at the St. Thomas. And he hasn't been falling-down drunk in almost a month."

Really, she thought, it wouldn't be right to leave Bowie out. "I'm willing to take a chance on him if you are. But I do worry a little about him giving Glory a bad time…."

"Ask her what she thinks. If she says she can't deal with the idea of him being there, we won't invite him."

"I'll call her." She dared to reach out, to touch his beard-stubbled cheek, to trace the shape of his ear.

He whispered her name. She lifted her lips to him.

The kiss they shared was achingly sweet—but too soon, he was pulling away. "Good night…" He rolled so he was facing the far wall and tugged the covers up over his shoulders.

"Good night," she said softly to his back, wanting to reach out for him again, to slip her arms around him, nuzzle his neck, rub her body against him until he turned to her once more.

But she restrained herself. The guy had just put in a sixteen-hour day. It was perfectly understandable that he was too tired to take her in his arms and love her doubts away.

Brand and Chastity both said they'd love to come to Old Tony's Fourth of July birthday celebration. Angie called Glory and asked what she'd think of them inviting Bowie.

"Invite him," Glory said without hesitation. "He's your brother-in-law—and he *has* been staying sober lately. He should be okay."

So it was decided. Bowie got an invitation, too.

At eight in the morning on the Fourth, Stella and Rose arrived at Angie's door.

"Will you look at this beautiful day?" Rose announced as Angie let them inside. The two commandeered the kitchen while Brett and Little Tony trekked in the endless bags of groceries, the bowls and platters and serving utensils.

Trista, Clarice and Dani appeared at eleven, bearing more food and more equipment, including several coolers and a couple of barbecue grills. Angie's dad, who always ran the grills, got busy setting up his cooking area. Brett was everywhere, finding anything the women needed, giving Little Tony a hand with the grills.

They all took a break at noon and went over to Main Street to watch the annual Fourth of July town parade, returning by one to continue the preparations.

At one-thirty Anthony and Gracie drove up with Baby Tony and a truckload of crushed ice, beer and wine, sodas and fruit drinks. They set to work filling the coolers. Trista's and Clarice's husbands, Donny and Mike, who rarely attended family events, even showed up at a quarter of two and pitched in moving picnic tables around.

By two-thirty in the afternoon, when the guest of honor appeared to cries of "Happy Birthday, Tony," the party was in full swing. The family sprawled through the house, spilled out to the deck and the patio below it.

All the kids wanted to go swimming. Matthew, ten, and the older of Clarice's two boys, volunteered to take them all down to the beach.

"I'll watch 'em, Mom. I'll watch 'em real good."

Clarice laughed. "Oh, I'll just bet you will."

"Aw, Mom. Come on. We wanna go swimmin'…"

So Clarice and Trista both put on their swimsuits and herded the kids down to the beach.

By then, Angie's dad had the grills going on the patio. Delicious aromas of grilling sausage and chicken filled the air.

Lucia and Petra, Angie's two still-single sisters who attended Cal State in Sacramento, had taken time off from their summer jobs to come to the party. They sat up on the deck with Brand and competed for his attention, laughing and sharing stories of their grown-up city-girl lives.

Chastity came with Alyosha. He joined the knot of men hanging around the grills, while Brett's mom headed for the kitchen to see what she could do to help. As it happened, Rose was just then opening a bottle of Old Tony's blackberry wine. Chastity said she'd love a glass. She had more than one. So did Rose and Stella. The three women whispered and laughed together, having such a fine time they forgot to watch the roast-pepper-and-Mozzarella crostini. The kitchen filled with smoke and the smoke alarm went off.

Angie ran around the main floor opening all the windows as her mom, her aunt and her mother-in-law, fighting shared fits of hysterical laughter, somehow managed to whip the smoking crostini from the oven, toss it in the sink and turn the cold water on it.

Bowie came at a little after four. Morose, but clearly sober, he drank Dr. Pepper and wandered around looking glum, eventually going down to the river for a swim. A little later, he reappeared on the deck—and headed straight for Glory, who was sitting on the long built-in bench beneath the railing with the sleeping Johnny in her arms.

It was a breath-held kind of moment. Everyone just knew there would be trouble.

Brand's easy smile faded and Petra and Lucia stopped chattering. Dani and Gracie, who were flitting around the picnic tables getting everything just right for the big birthday meal, cast worried glances at each other. Even Nonna Baldovino, who sat in a nice padded lawn chair smiling benignly and sipping a gin and tonic, suddenly looked tense.

Angie, emerging from the great room through the open French doors, a bowl of chips in either hand, stopped stock-still and wondered what had possessed her to even consider inviting Bowie.

"How's he doing?" Bowie asked, tipping his head at his sleeping son and shocking them all by sounding almost shy.

"He's good." Glory's soft mouth quivered. She looked down at Johnny, then back up at his father. And then, cautiously, she gave Bowie a smile. "Real good."

Even though she smiled, Glory looked…so very sad, Angie thought. For herself. For the golden-haired man looming over her. For the baby they had made. Angie understood that sadness, the sadness of loving when loving somehow wasn't enough.

Love…

Angie knew it then, at that moment, as she recognized her sister's sadness and felt that sadness in herself.

I'm in love with my husband. I'm in love with Brett….

In love…

Oh, yeah. She couldn't deny it anymore. She was in love with Brett—crazy, madly, wildly, deeply.

In love.

Too bad Brett had told her from the first that he'd

never be in love with her. Too bad she'd agreed with him, promised him she wanted what he wanted from their lives together: sanity and normalness, nothing wild or extreme.

No emotional danger…

What a mess, Angie thought. *It should be so right— and yet it's all completely wrong.*

Glory, her shining gaze still locked on Bowie, offered softly, "You want to hold him?"

Bowie speared his fingers through his shaggy, still wet hair. "Uh. Yeah. I'd like that. I'd like it a lot."

Glory indicated the space beside her. "Okay, then. Sit here."

Bowie dropped to the bench. Glory rose and, with great care, handed him down his son to hold. Johnny yawned and opened his eyes. He caught Bowie's thumb in his plump baby fist and made a happy cooing sound.

"He's so damn small…." Bowie's voice was rough with wonder.

Glory chuckled low. "Hey, he's huge compared to the day he was born…" Her voice trailed off. Slowly she turned and saw everyone watching them. She rolled her eyes. "Okay, everybody. Nothing thrilling's gonna happen here. You can all stop staring now."

That broke the spell. In a breathless rush of voices, they all started talking at once. A sweet trill of a laugh escaped Petra, a response to some remark Brand had made. Ice cubes clinked in Nonna's glass as she delicately sipped her cocktail. Gracie told Dani, "Well, I'd say this table looks as ready as it's going to get…."

Still, for the life of her, Angie couldn't move. She stayed rooted in place between the open French doors, clutching the bowls of chips, struck speechless by what she'd just realized.

In love. Oh, my God. I'm crazy in love with Brett….

It seemed so huge and terrible and frighteningly new—at the same time as she had to admit that, deep down, she'd known it all along, been lying all along: to Brett and to herself.

"Angie, you okay?" Dani was looking at her sideways.

"Uh, yeah. Fine. Terrific." Yet another lie, but a tiny one this time, a lie that was nothing compared to the whopper she'd been telling herself for two months now. Gathering every ounce of determination she possessed, she ordered her shaky legs to take one step and then another. "Here you go." She passed the bowls of chips to Dani. Then she leaned over the deck railing and called to her father below at the grills. "Dad, how's it going?"

He glanced up at her. "Bring those platters down here and let's get it all on the table." Brett stood at his side.

"Be right down," Angie promised, her gaze drawn like a magnet to the tall, broad-shouldered man she had married, the man she loved with all her heart.

Brett gave her a quick smile—and then looked away.

No use staring when he wasn't staring back. She pushed off from the railing, turning for the house.

And whipped right back around again when a woman's desperate scream erupted from down by the river. "Help! Oh, my God, Matthew! Somebody, help!"

Chapter Nine

As the frantic screams tore through the mountain air, Brett plunked his beer on the nearest flat surface and took off, racing to the street, across it and down the sandy path to the river's edge in seconds flat.

Clarice was still screaming as she dived into the water. Beneath the high rocks on the other side, in the natural pool formed where the current caught and eddied, the limp body of her older son floated loosely, turning a slow circle.

Trista tried to follow her. Brett caught up with her in time and grabbed her arm. "Watch the other kids."

"Oh, God," she screeched, blinking as if waking from a trance, and wildly glancing around at the other kids, any one of whom, left unsupervised, might end up caught in the swift current and swept downstream. "Of course," she cried. "I will. Okay…"

Brett paused long enough to shuck off his shoes. He dived. It was cold enough to bring a gasp, but not to slow him down. He swam for all he was worth. The current tugged at his clothes, dragging at him. He only swam harder, reaching Clarice and the unconscious child in no time.

Sobbing, calling her son's name, she had Matthew turned face-up by then. She struggled to keep his mouth and nose above water. As best he could right there on the spot, Brett assessed the boy's condition. He couldn't see any chest movement, but the boy's skin color still looked pretty good—too pale, but not yet turned blue. Near his hairline, the kid sported a nasty contusion.

"He dived too deep," cried Clarice, telling Brett what he'd already figured out. "He hit his head on the rocks underneath…."

"Pass him to me."

Miraculously, Clarice did as he'd told her. Brett got an arm under the unconscious boy's small torso, bracing his limp body high enough that his head was clear of the water. Stroking out with his free arm, he took off for the other side.

It wasn't all that far. In a few long strokes, he could lower his feet. Once he was upright, he took a couple more steps and the rushing water was waist-high. He didn't squander the crucial extra seconds it would have taken to carry the kid up to the beach. He simply switched his grip so he held the boy from underneath, checked for obstructions to the airway, found none, and started mouth-to-mouth, right there in the water. He took care not to tip the head too far back, and to get a good seal over the mouth each time. The object was to deliver slow, gentle breaths at four-second intervals.

By the third breath the kid started breathing on his own—followed immediately by hard coughing and sputtering. Only then, did Brett hoist the boy against his chest and forge onto dry land.

The worried crowd on the beach parted so Brett could carry Matthew to the nest of blankets Angie had ready and waiting. He knew without having to ask that she would have already called 9-1-1.

Carefully, Brett dropped to a crouch, set the boy down, rolled him gently to his stomach and into the recovery position—top arm and leg at right angles to the body, head tilting back, chin jutting forward—so the fluids would drain as he expelled them.

Swallowed water started coming up, along with the kid's breakfast and lunch. As soon as that was over, Brett and Angie eased him onto a clean blanket. Angie covered him as Dani and Gracie grabbed a couple of plastic buckets and cleaned up the mess.

"It's going to be all right," Brett promised Clarice and her husband Mike, as the couple moved in closer to kneel by their son. "I'll have to check that bump on his head, but it looks to me like he's going to pull out of this just fine."

A few feet away, Stella sent up a prayer of gratitude to the Holy Virgin. Rose cried, "Thank God you were here, Brett."

A murmur of agreement went up. "Yeah, Brett."

"Good going, Brett."

"What did we ever do without you…?"

Brett's gaze collided with Angie's. "Our hero." She mouthed the words—the same words she'd said the day after they were married, when he found little Stephanie in that cabinet under the stairs.

That day, she'd looked up at him with stars in her eyes. Now she just looked sad—and then quickly turned away to tuck the blanket more snuggly around the shivering child.

By the time the EMTs arrived, Brett had already examined Matthew's injury and asked him a few questions to confirm that he was thinking clearly. The techs waited while Brett ran the usual checks for strength, balance, coordination, reflexes and sensation. All were normal. No need to send the kid to the hospital.

The EMTs took off. Since the danger was passed, people started wandering back up the hill again, headed for the house and the almost-ready birthday meal. Brett spent a couple of minutes with Clarice and Mike, explaining the dangers of post-concussive syndrome and telling them what signs to watch for, reassuring them again that he didn't think there was anything to worry about, but they should make sure that Matthew took it easy for the next couple of days.

"Come on everybody…." It was Rose, at the top of the trail leading down from the street. "We're about to put the food on the table."

The stragglers started up the path. Matthew, on his feet by then and wrapped in a blanket, strode along beside his father in the center of the small group.

Brett hung back a little, though his dripping chinos and wet shirt clung to him uncomfortably and he really needed to get up to the house and into clean, dry clothes. He watched the others as they moved away from him. They were all chattering and laughing now, enjoying the rush of relief that follows an averted disaster.

He didn't realize that he was hoping Angie might pause and look for him—until she did, at the top of the path.

She stopped. And she waited.

He stared up at her, those feelings he couldn't deal with rising within him: lust and yearning. Possessiveness. Fear.

It wasn't good. It wasn't…the way he'd planned for it to be.

And how the hell long was he going to stand here, dripping wet with soggy sand between his toes, staring longingly at his wife like a lovesick, hopeless fool?

Brett swore under his breath, turned, scooped up his shoes, and hurried to catch up with her.

* * *

Well after midnight, when everyone finally went home, Angie and Brett sat out on the deck in the cool darkness, listening to the occasional explosions of illegal firecrackers down by the river and the faint strains of music from the town hall, where the merchant's association was putting on their annual Fourth of July dance.

Angie shivered as the night breeze found its way under the sweater she'd thrown over her shoulders. Tugging the sweater closer, she tried to figure out where to begin. How to tell him she loved him in the way she'd promised that she wouldn't.

How to get him to see…

What?

That it would be okay? That they would work it out? That there was nothing wrong with loving someone as passionately and completely as she loved him.

That all she wanted in the world was to find a way to bridge this strange distance that yawned between them, scarily wider every day?

He said, "It was a good party."

She said, "Yeah. They all had a great time." She added dryly, "Even if Matthew did almost drown."

He stared off into the middle distance for a moment. Then he muttered, "Your aunt Stella took me aside."

Surprise, surprise. "Let me guess. About having our marriage blessed by the church."

"She says it's important and you need to talk to Father Delahunty."

"I know. I will...." *Brett, I love you. In the way I told you I wouldn't love you. But I can't help it. I do—and really, what is so wrong with that? To me, it feels like a good thing, the* greatest *thing....*

He stood. "Ready for bed?"

Her courage deserted her. Which was just more proof of how bad things had gotten. By now, it seemed forever ago, those lovely faraway days when she'd felt that she could tell him anything, that he would listen, and no matter what she revealed, he'd understand.

Maybe, she found herself thinking, tonight wasn't such a good time, after all. Maybe some other time. Maybe tomorrow.

She got up and followed him in.

In bed, she cuddled up close to him. He kissed her on the top of her head and whispered, "Good night."

An hour later she was still wide awake, staring at the ceiling, thinking how they hadn't made love in over a week. They couldn't go on like this: not really talking, not making love, just kind of moving through their lives by rote, kind of getting through the days.

Together—and yet, in all the ways that really counted, so far apart.

And maybe, the more she thought about it, that was what scared her the most. That they *could* go on like this.

That nothing would change.

* * *

The following Monday at the diner, once they'd gotten their drinks and given Charlene their order, Glory announced, "Bowie's left town."

Angie took a moment to digest that stunning piece of news. Then she asked carefully, "You mean, like...for good?"

"Well, let me put it this way. If he comes back, it's not gonna be for a long time. He came over to the B and B last night to say goodbye to me and Johnny—and Chastity, too."

"I shouldn't ask...."

"Oh, go ahead."

"Well, was he...?"

"Drunk? Nope. He was stone-cold sober. He's been sober for over a month, believe it or not. Long enough, he told me, to start thinking more clearly about everything that's not working in his life. Did you know he's been going to AA meetings down in Nevada City?"

"No—but that's good. It's a big step."

Glory nodded, her eyes misty. "He told me he needs a new start. I can't say I blame him...."

Angie reached across the table to brush her sister's hand. "You miss him already."

Glory dabbed at her eyes with her napkin. "Yeah. I guess I do. But you know what? I think it's a good thing, the *right* thing, for him. He's a little like Buck, you know?"

"Yeah. I do know. Bowie needs to get out in the world, to start over in a new place where his reputation as the craziest Bravo boy doesn't dog his every move."

Glory caught her lower lip between her teeth. "And, Angie, there's more...."

Angie had the strangest, sinking feeling. She gulped. "What? Tell me."

"Well, I'm thinkin' a fresh start sounds pretty good to me, too." Her sister leaned closer. "I've talked to B.J. Did you know she had her baby? A little boy. Joseph James. B.J.'s got a big-time career. She needs a nanny, someone she can count on to love little Joey like her own...."

Angie's mouth felt so dry, as if she'd stuffed a wad of cotton in there. She gulped to ease that dryness. "New York City? You and Johnny are moving to New York City?"

"Angie, try to understand."

"Oh. Well. Of course, I understand."

"You don't look like you understand. You look like you're about to cry."

Angie swallowed again. Hard. "Well, I'm not."

"You have to see. It's a good thing for me. I'll get a big salary, and I'll have minimal living expenses, since I'll be moving in with B.J. and Buck. Johnny and I will get full medical. *And* Buck and B.J. are going to pay for me to take college courses online. By the time Johnny's old enough for kindergarten, I'll have myself a real career...."

It *was* a good deal. No doubt about it. "You're right." Angie forced a smile. "It sounds terrific. And I know you and B.J. are best friends. You'll have someone you can talk to…."

"I'll be with family. I mean, think about it. Joey and Johnny are cousins."

"That's right—and, um, you surprised me, at first. But the more I get used to the idea, the more I see what a terrific opportunity this is going to be for you."

Glory braced her forearms on the table, laced her fingers together and looked down at them. "Mamma and Aunt Stella will have a fit. *All* of them will. I can just hear Great-Grandpa Tony now, yellin' at me, calling me a damn fool…."

Angie spoke briskly. "You gonna let that stop you?"

Glory glanced up, a naughty gleam in her eyes. "Heck, no. I see my chance and I'm takin' it."

"Good for you."

Glory reached across the table again and squeezed Angie's arm. "As far as going, I'm sorry for one thing and one thing only. That's having to leave *you*. I know how much you need me now, with all the confusion in your poor mind and heart. I know, since you came back to town, that I'm the only one in the whole family you can talk to."

Angie opened her mouth to argue that she wasn't the least confused. She shut it before one lying word got out. "You're right," she confessed. "You are the only one around here I can talk to." *Now that Brett and I are hardly speaking, that is.*

Glory was dabbing her eyes again. "Oh, I'm gonna

miss you. We're gonna have one huge long-distance phone bill."

"We'll have to get one of those discount calling plans...."

"Oh, yeah. Absolutely."

They were straining across the table toward each other, clutching each other's hands, when Charlene approached with their sandwiches. "Light on the mayo," she said gently. "Extra French fries." The sisters sank back into their separate sides of the booth and Charlene set their plates before them.

"Thanks." Glory dabbed her eyes with her napkin again.

"'Preciate that." Angie bravely sniffed.

Charlene fished a travel pack of tissues from her apron and plunked it on the end of the table. "Here you go. Wipe up. And remember, there's never a night so dark that morning doesn't come around eventually." With a blinding smile, she turned and trotted back to the counter again.

Angie took a tissue and handed one to Glory. "When are you leaving?"

"Thursday."

"So soon..."

"No sense hangin' around here when I know where I'm going."

"Before you leave..."

"Yeah?"

They were leaning close again. Angie whispered, "I

have to tell you. I have to…get it off my chest to some-one."

Glory sent a series of sharp glances around the diner—and then leaned even closer. "It's okay. No one's listening…"

"It's Brett…"

"Well, of course it is."

"Glory, I love him. I love him so much. I am long-gone crazy in love with my husband."

Glory wasn't especially impressed. "Well, of course you are. Now tell me something I don't already know."

Angie groaned—realized she'd done it a little too loud, and took extra care to pitch her voice at a confi-dential level. "You don't get it. Falling passionately in love with Brett wasn't the plan. We got married because we *weren't* in love."

Glory gaped. "Uh. Run that one by me again."

How to explain? "We're, you know, well-suited. It was a reasonable, logical decision we made, to get married, to start a life together. Being in love didn't even enter into it."

Glory waved a hand as if batting away some pesky insect. "Oh, come on. You went to work for him on a Monday—and four nights later, you eloped with him."

"Haven't we been over this before? It's not like we were strangers. I've known Brett all my life."

"But you hadn't seen him in a decade. Angie, hon. Here's a hot flash for you. Logic and reason had nothin' to do with it. There was no *reason* for you to do something so crazy as run off out of nowhere and marry Brett Bravo. Not unless the two of you were insanely in love—which you are."

"Uh-uh. No. It wasn't about love. At least not *that* kind of love."

"*That* kind?"

"You know, the passionate kind, the *dangerous* kind."

"Okay. Say I go along, just for the sake of argument. If you didn't marry him because you're out of your mind in love with him…they why?"

"We…got along so well. We were so comfortable with each other. We could talk for hours and hours, say anything to each other. We, um, really *liked* each other. We were each other's best friends."

"And then…?"

"And then we had sex."

"Huh? But I thought you said…I mean, you told me right after you got married that the sex was—"

"Incredible," Angie finished for her. "Fabulous. The best I've ever had."

"Wait a minute."

"Yeah?"

"You're sayin' that sex with Brett was even better than with that Harley-ridin', two-timin', bank-account stealing, ex-boyfriend of yours?"

"Oh, yeah. And I didn't think there *was* better sex than what I had with Jody."

"Well, great, then. Even if Brett's got those intimacy issues we talked about, it could be worse."

"Oh, I don't think so."

"Look. Count your blessings. You've both got real jobs. Brett has no problem stayin' sober. He maybe doesn't talk your ear off anymore, but at least he treats you right—and you can't wait to get home at night and jump each other's bones."

"Well, not exactly."

"*Why* not exactly?"

"Well, first of all, I hate that I feel like I lost my best friend."

"Oh, well. Yeah," Glory had to agree. "I know. I can see that. But you've still got—"

Angie cut in. "Guess again."

"Oh, no. Not the hot sex?"

"Yeah. Pouf. Gone."

"But…why?"

"Oh, Glory. I just don't know."

Glory screwed the top off the ketchup bottle and pounded the bottom until the contents came out in a river, drowning her French fries. "You need to have a long talk with your husband."

"Believe me, I've tried." Angie took the bottle and drowned her own French fries.

Glory insisted, "Try harder—and you *have* told him you're in love him, in spite of all that wimpy stuff about *reason* and *logic,* right?"

Angie screwed the lid back on the bottle, set it aside—and looked down at her lunch.

"Right?" Glory asked again. Angie kept staring at

her sandwich. "Hey. Forget that BLT for a minute. Look here, in my eyes."

Angie dragged her head up. "Okay. What?"

"I'm getting the picture. It is not pretty."

"Oh, Glory…"

"You haven't told him, have you?"

"Well, I keep meaning to, I honestly do."

"Do it."

"You make it sound so simple."

"It is. Tell him somethin' good. Open with 'I'm in with love you, Brett.' And let things take their natural course from there."

Chapter Ten

At four-thirty that afternoon, Marla Pinkley, who owned and ran Marla's House of Beauty two doors down from the St. Thomas, on Main, went into labor with her second child. Brett sent her to the hospital in Grass Valley and then went to meet her there.

He got back home after midnight. Angie, in bed in the dark, doing her usual ceiling-staring routine, heard him come in.

"You awake?" he whispered when he climbed into bed with her.

How could she not be? She'd been waiting for hours—to tell him, to make him see. "Yeah. I'm awake."

"Marla had a girl. Six pounds, seven ounces. They named her Jessica Louise."

"Pretty name…" *Start with* I'm in love with you, Brett. *Oh, right. Easy for Glory to say….*

"Marla told me that Bowie's left town. Walked out on his job at the St. Thomas. Just like that. Can you believe it? What a fool. I stopped by to see Ma before I came home. She confirmed it. Bowie's run off."

Really, wasn't he being a little hard on his brother? "Your mother said that—that he'd *run off?*"

"Well, no. She didn't put it that way. But that *is* what he did."

"I disagree. He left town, yes. Because he wants a new start."

Brett canted up on an elbow and frowned down at her. She could make out his furrowed brow even in the darkness. "How do you know?"

"Glory told me at lunch today."

Brett swore and dropped back to his pillow. He spoke to the ceiling. "You knew since lunch? You never said a word to me."

Oh, yeah. Like you're so easy to talk to lately. Wearily, she explained, "The time never seemed right. We were busy at the clinic. And then you got the call from Marla at four-thirty."

"You should have told me."

Why argue the point? "Yeah. I guess I should have. Sorry."

"Well. It's okay." He said it like it was some major concession.

She held back a snide remark. "Glory's leaving, too," she said before he could accuse her of not telling him about that.

He turned over, away from her, and pulled the covers up. "Yeah." His voice lost volume—because he was speaking to the far wall. "Ma told me. She said Buck and B.J. will put her through college."

"I think it's a good deal for her...."

"Your family will freak."

"Too bad. Glory has to do what's right for her and Johnny now." Well, at least they were talking. Even in the dark, with him facing the other way, at least they were having an actual conversation.... "Brett?"

He didn't answer.

"Brett?"

Only soft, shallow breathing came from his side of the bed.

Okay. So she'd have to wait till tomorrow night to tell him how she was madly in love with him.

Angie stopped by the B and B at lunchtime the next day. Chastity told her that Glory was at work, pushing the maid's cart around the rambling old house, cleaning the rooms.

"She's upstairs." Chastity tipped her head toward the staircase. "Tell her I said she should take a break and visit with her sister while she still can." Brett's mom looked kind of wistful.

Angie said, "I'm going to miss her."

Chastity nodded. "Oh, me, too. She's a daughter to me—not to mention, she's the mother of my grandson."

"She loves you, too. Lots."

"I know—now, listen. I made up some tuna salad. You two go on in the kitchen and help yourselves. I'll keep my eye on Johnny."

"Well?" Glory asked when they sat down with their sandwiches. "Did you tell him?"

Angie had to admit that she hadn't. "—Yet. But I will. Tonight."

"You'd better."

Angie laughed. "You are getting so pushy."

"I want to know that you're gonna be okay, before I take off to live three thousand miles away."

"Oh, Glory. I'll be okay, whatever happens. And if I really need your advice, you know I'll be calling."

"You'd better."

Angie gazed across the kitchen table at her baby sis. "I can't believe I got through ten whole years without you to talk to."

"We have to make sure that never happens again."

"Oh, yeah. We definitely do." Angie picked up a triangle of tuna sandwich and nibbled the crust. "So did Mamma have a heart attack when you told her that you're leaving?"

Now it was Glory's turn to look everywhere but at her sister.

Angie put the sandwich down. "You haven't told the family yet."

"I'm going to. Today. Soon as I finish cleaning the rooms."

"How about if I go up to the house with you, provide a little moral support?"

"Uh-uh. I can handle it."

"You're sure?"

"Come on. You know me. I got the Dellazola shouting gene. They shout. I shout louder—and you better tell Brett you love him. Tonight. Try a romantic approach. You know, a couple of good steaks. Wine. Candles on the table…"

"What's the occasion?" Brett pulled back his chair and sat down at the dining area table. Angie had set it with the good china and opened that nice bottle of Pinot Noir she'd bought during her last trip to Grass Valley for groceries.

She put the platter of steaks on the table and filled his wineglass. "Oh, I just felt like sitting at the big table for a change…"

He tasted the wine, nodded his approval. "Those steaks look good."

"Help yourself." She took the chair opposite him, filled her own glass and then pretended to sip from it.

Lately, her stomach had been acting up a little. Just the smell of the wine made her feel slightly queasy.

Or maybe it was only nerves. The big moment was almost upon her. This time, she was determined not to chicken out. She was telling her husband she loved him if it killed her to do it—or *him,* she found herself thinking.

Of the two of us, it's more likely to kill him.

And, really, how bizarre was that? A twenty-first-century American marriage where the wife didn't dare tell her husband she loved him.

That was strange.

That was so far from normal as to be almost laughable. And wasn't that what Brett claimed he wanted: normal?

Oh, yeah. Normal, above all.

"You closed all the blinds," Brett said as he forked himself up a big steak from the platter.

"It's still light out." She tipped her head toward the two slim, glowing tapers in the center of the table. "And I felt like having candles…."

Brett took a warm dinner roll, broke it open and buttered it. She watched the fragrant steam rise from the white center.

Should she let him finish his steak before she told him? Make sure he got his nourishment before laying it on him?

Oh, this was ridiculous.

She was ridiculous.

What was the big deal? It was only five little words,

after all—*I'm in love with you*—six, if you counted the contraction as two. How tough could it be?

"Ahem. Brett?"

He set down his butter knife. "Yeah?"

"I'm in—" And the phone rang. Angie stifled a cry of frustration as Brett nudged back his chair. "Stop," she commanded as the phone trilled out another ring. "Don't answer it. Just let it ring."

"It could be an emergency." He got up anyway as she wondered what had possessed her to marry a doctor. The phone rang once more while he was checking the display. "It's your parents."

"I'll call them back later. Come on, sit down."

"You're sure?"

"I have never been so sure about anything in my entire life."

With a shrug, he returned to the table and took his seat. The machine picked up and Brett's recorded voice instructed the caller to leave a message. There was a beep.

And her mother started shouting. "Angela Marie, pick up! Are you there? Pick up right now."

Brett arched an eyebrow. "She sounds pretty frantic."

"That doesn't necessarily mean there's anything to be frantic about."

"Angela." Aunt Stella's voice. "Angela, you call us back the minute you get this message."

Now Brett was looking at her reproachfully.

"Okay, okay." She shoved back her chair, threw down her napkin, stomped over to the peninsula, grabbed the phone and growled into it, "I'm here. What?"

"Oh, you *know* what," her mother accused. "It's Glory."

"She's leaving town." Aunt Stella was outraged. "She's taking that innocent baby and she's moving to…" Stella paused for effect, and then finished, *"New York City,"* in a tone of pure horror.

"Thousands of miles from her family," wailed Rose.

"You better talk to her, Angie!" Great-Grandpa Tony shouted from somewhere in the background.

Stella sneered, "She said no to Bowie so many times that he's given up all hope and gone wandering in the wilderness. She wouldn't let that poor, misguided man make things right, wouldn't give that poor baby an honest name."

"Angie, you talk to her!" Great-Grandpa Tony yelled again.

"We have to stop her," cried Rose.

"Yes," agreed Stella. "We have to convince her she's doing a terrible thing."

Angie realized there was no way she'd ever get through to them on the phone—well, she probably wouldn't get through to them no matter what. But she figured she owed it to her sister to give it a try.

"I'll be right over," she said.

"Yes!" cried Rose. "We need to tell you what to say to her."

"Ten minutes." She hung up before they could all start shouting again.

"Trouble over Glory leaving?" Well, at least Brett sounded sympathetic.

"How did you guess?"

"I told you they would freak when they found out."

She went back to the table and blew out the candles. So much for the romantic approach. "Enjoy your dinner."

He had the grace to look sheepish. "I'll go with you."

She put up a hand before he could rise from his chair. "It won't help. And they're pretty wound up over there. You could end up with permanent damage to your eardrums."

"Call them back. Tell them you're in the middle of dinner and you'll be over later."

By then, she didn't feel much like eating, anyway. Her poor stomach churned. And the whole point was that she and Brett not be interrupted while she told him how she felt and tried to bridge the gap between them. If she told him now, it would be, *I love you like crazy— and I've got to go.*

Uh-uh. She'd have to try again later. Maybe after she got home.

She said, "The longer it takes me to get over there, the more they'll work themselves into a frenzy. I'm better off going now."

* * *

Her mother, her aunt and her great-grandpa Tony were waiting for her out on the porch. They all started in at once as she came up the steps. Rose cried and Stella lectured.

Old Tony kept shouting, "You got to get through to that girl. You're the only one she'll listen to, the only one who can talk some sense into her…"

"Let's go inside," she told them with a tight smile— and pulled open the screen and went in, giving them no choice but to follow.

Which they did, trailing after her, all three of them babbling, loud and nonstop, into the living room.

"It's not good for the baby…."

"Glory has to learn to be responsible…."

"She belongs here, at home, where her family can watch out for her…."

In the living room, Angie took a chair. She folded her hands in her lap and waited for the three of them to wind down. It took a while. She spotted her father as he stuck his head around the door frame from the central hall—and then instantly retreated up the stairs.

For a Dellazola, her dad was the quiet type. He'd lay down the law now and then, but he didn't like competing with the rest of them. If he wanted to give you orders, to tell you what you should do, he'd wait until he could get you alone.

Eventually, her aunt Stella commanded, "Angela. Tell us. Tell us you'll talk to her."

Finally something that required an answer. "No," Angie said. It was the first word she'd uttered since she entered the house.

And as she'd hoped it might, it gave the three of them pause. They gaped at her.

Old Tony sputtered back to life first. "What in hell do you mean, no?"

"I mean, I'm *not* going to talk to Glory about staying here in town."

Again, they all started yelling at once. Angie let them.

She kept her mouth shut until her mother finally demanded, "Why? Why won't you talk to her?"

And she told them. "I don't think staying here in town is working for her. Buck and B.J. have offered her a terrific opportunity, a chance for a new start, a chance to be able to take good care of her baby—and go to college at the same time. I'm completely behind her in this. I support her all the way. She's an adult and it's her right to make her own choices in life."

"But—"

Angie put up a hand before Stella could get going again. Her aunt surprised her by shutting her mouth. "Leave her alone," Angie said. "Let her find her own way. She's going to New York, whether you like it or not. You won't change her mind—all you'll do is make it so she dreads the very thought of ever coming back."

Her mother let out a soft cry, then—and sank to the sofa. Stella remained blessedly silent.

And Great-Grandpa Tony just shook his head.

That was when Angie knew she'd finally gotten through to them.

At home, Brett's place at the table was cleared off and he was nowhere in sight. He'd left a note on the counter that said he'd gotten a call.

Another emergency. She felt a flare of resentment—and reminded herself that handling emergencies was part of his job.

Angie plopped a cold steak on her plate, served herself some asparagus and a mound of wild rice. She heated the food in the microwave and sat down to eat.

She was proud of the way she'd handled things at her mother's house. For the first time in her life, she'd succeeded in getting her mother, her aunt and her great-grandfather to stop shouting long enough to see things a different way.

It was a big step. It gave her hope for her future relationship with her family.

Too bad she wasn't doing as well with her husband.

That night he came home later than ever. She had no idea when, exactly, because she was sound asleep by then.

The next day…well, the moment never seemed right.

Thursday, Angie took the morning off to drive Glory

and Johnny to Reno so they could catch their plane. During the ride, Glory spouted constant encouragements.

"Just tell him, Angie. Just get the words out. That's all you need to do."

Angie wasn't so sure about that, but she nodded and said she would, and kept her eyes on the twisting road ahead.

At the airport, she hugged her sister and kissed her nephew's plump, velvety cheek.

"Here are my numbers." Glory pressed a folded piece of paper into Angie's hand. "Call me. I mean it. Anytime you need to talk."

Angie promised that she would and waved them off through the security checkpoint. As she turned to head for her car, she realized she'd never in her life felt so alone.

Her sister, the one she'd come to trust with all her secrets, was flying off to a new life on the other side of the continent. And she no longer knew how to talk to her husband.

It was worse, somehow, than in San Francisco, when Jody had betrayed her, beat her black and blue and stole all her money. At least she'd always known that Jody was dangerous.

But Brett...

She'd been happy with Brett. For a few short, shining weeks. Now she knew what happiness could be, the lack of it seemed somehow all the more painful.

And come on. Really. As if telling Brett she was in love with him was going to change a damn thing....

But still, her sister's words echoed reproachfully in her brain. *Just tell him. Just get the words out.*

So all right. Fair enough. Tonight. She would tell him tonight. No backing out, no putting it off.

If he got an emergency call, she'd stay up no matter how late he came home. If her family just *had* to talk to her—too bad. They could wait.

Nothing.

Nothing would keep her from saying the words.

The minute they got home from work, she was hitting him with it.

Chapter Eleven

"Please," Angie said. "Sit down. I really have to talk to you."

Brett knew he had no choice. He could see it in her eyes. She wasn't putting up with any more evasions.

They were having a "talk" and they were having it now.

Yeah, he *had* been avoiding any "talks" lately. He couldn't see the percentage in hashing it all out. As far as he was concerned, the problem wasn't anything talking would solve.

He was, after all, living his worst nightmare. He had it and he had it bad.

For Angie.

Morning, noon and night and every moment in

between, she was all he could think about. He adored her. He was terrified of losing her. Sometimes he wondered about that guy named Jody, the rotten S.O.B. who'd messed her over.

Was she still in love with that bastard? Was Brett just second best?

She'd promised him she was over that guy. Still, he wondered.

And he despised himself for wondering. He hated that it mattered so damn much.

This wasn't…normal. This wasn't reasonable. Or balanced.

And damn it. All he'd ever wanted was a normal, reasonable, emotionally balanced life.

He didn't want to be like his mother had been over his father. Like Bowie was for Glory. Like *he* had been for Lisa once.

Brett liked to live his life in moderation.

And what he felt for Angie now…

Not moderate in the least. It was hotter, wilder, more extreme even than the way he'd felt about Lisa.

Time, he kept telling himself. Time would take care of it. Time would ease the hunger. Time would dull the need.

He was, after all, a doctor. He understood the biological imperatives. Overwhelming attraction meant a high likelihood of surrender to the sexual act. The sexual act assured the proliferation of the species.

This madness had a purpose and that purpose was mating. Frequent mating. But even Mother Nature didn't expect anyone to live in a never-ending state of sexual arousal.

The studies he'd read predicted that wild sexual attraction, the "honeymoon glow" faded into something milder, more reasonable, within four months to a year. All he had to do was wait this agony out. He'd be free of this constant *needing* by next May at the latest.

Then, finally, he and Angie could settle into the kind of life they both wanted: a comfortable life free of destructive emotional extremes.

Hell. Maybe he'd get lucky and four months would do it; this unbearable yearning would mellow by fall.

"Brett?"

He pushed the depressing thoughts away and met her waiting eyes. "Yeah?"

She indicated the sofa near the fieldstone fireplace. "Please."

He wished the phone would ring. It didn't.

He scoured his brain for some reason he *had* to leave. Now.

But no. Time to stop evading this issue. He didn't need to talk—didn't *want* to talk. But Angie did. She'd told him the night she married him that the thing she loved best about their relationship was the way she could tell him anything. It just wasn't right or fair for him to keep sidestepping her attempts to get through to him.

He trudged to the sofa and dropped into it. "Okay, Angie." He knew he sounded hostile as hell, so he strove for a milder tone. "What is it?"

She marched over and stood between him and the fireplace. "I…" She gulped. Her slim hands were fisted at her sides, the mouth he loved to kiss no more than a bleak line.

All at once he wondered if he'd completely misjudged her; if this was about something more than how they didn't *talk* anymore.

Something worse. Something unbearable…

Was she leaving him?

His gut tightened to a knot and the breath fled his chest. *Anything,* damn it to hell. *Anything* but that…

She said, "Um, Brett. I'm sorry if this upsets you. I know it's not what we planned, not what we agreed on, but—"

He could hardly get air, but somehow, he managed to blurt, "Angie. Oh, God. Don't say it."

"I have to."

He half rose from the sofa. "No…"

"Yeah. Oh, Brett. I'm in love with you. Just crazy in love with you. I know it's not what you want from me, but I can't help it. It's true."

It took maybe five seconds for her words to sink in. He sank to the sofa again and stared up at her, slack-jawed. "You, uh, what?"

She drew herself up. "I'm in love with you. Deeply. Completely. I'm sorry that it's not part of the plan, but I really am."

So. She wasn't leaving him, after all. She was only telling him that she felt for *him* what he felt for *her.*

He realized he could breathe again. *She was in love with him....*

Well, okay. He could live with that.

Though he hated to think of her suffering as he suffered, at least if she was good and gone on him, it was unlikely she would leave him. If they were lucky, they'd still be together when all this passion crap finally ran its course.

"It's okay," he said grimly. "I'm in love with you, too."

Now she was the one gaping. "But...you hardly talk to me anymore."

"This state I'm in..." He shrugged. "It's not real conducive to friendly conversation."

She backed up until her legs met the easy chair behind her. Slowly she lowered herself into it. "You're in love with me...and that makes it hard to talk to me?"

Why was that so difficult to understand? "Angie. When I'm around you, all I want to do is rip your clothes off and get inside you. And since I'm around you most of the time, my life is pretty much a living hell."

"Oh," she said after a moment. "Well." Her sweet mouth quivered—as if she couldn't decide whether to smile or to frown. "A living hell, huh?"

"All right," he said gruffly. "That's a little over the top. Let's just say it's distracting. In the extreme."

Her smooth brow furrowed. "But in the last couple of weeks, you hardly get near me. We haven't made love. You don't even kiss me...."

So okay. He'd been trying to exercise a little restraint, trying to prove to himself that he could get by without boinking his wife every five minutes. "I keep trying to tell myself that there are other things in life than sex. The only problem is, lately, I don't give a good damn about any of them."

She did smile, then. He watched the dimples appear in her cheeks and wanted to grab her and slam his mouth down on hers. "Well, Brett…"

"What?" The word came out ragged and low.

"It just seems so simple to me," she said sweetly. "We're married. We love each other. You want me. I want you. We should be doing…what comes naturally."

What comes naturally…

Erotic images flashed through his brain, all of them involving Angie, naked, doing *what comes naturally.*

Heat sluiced through him, hardening what he'd been trying to keep limp. He shifted on the sofa cushions. She must have known why. Her gaze slipped down—then shot up again to his face. He watched the warm color sweep up her smooth throat and flood her cheeks.

Why the hell not?

This whole abstinence thing wasn't working, anyway. Keeping away from her wasn't any better than grabbing her every time the mood struck. True, every time he had her, he only wanted her more. But when he denied himself, all he thought about was the moment when he would give in and take her.

So it didn't matter. He could take her at each and every opportunity.

Or say no. Either way, he would be thinking of her constantly, longing for her all the time.

At least he felt good when he was making love with her. At least, when he had her in his arms, all was right in his world.

She rose from the chair with the same slow, graceful care as when she'd lowered herself into it. "Please, Brett...don't close yourself off from me. Kiss me. Make love to me. I've...well, I've just missed you so much...."

All the blood seemed to pool in his groin. His heart beat out a hard rhythm of need.

And the damn blinds were open....

She read his mind. "I'll do it. Stay right there." She took off, zipping around the great room, tugging on cords.

He watched her, admiring the shape of her bottom in those white jeans she wore to the clinic, achingly aware of the roundness of her breasts. Even beneath her loose nurse's tunic, those breasts taunted him.

In seconds, the room lay in shadow. No one out there could see in.

It was just the two of them.

At last.

She returned to him.

With great effort, he kept himself from reaching for her. Yet. He commanded in a voice rough with arousal, "Take everything off."

She did—fast—kicking off her flat-soled shoes, whipping that tunic over her head, unclasping her bra and shrugging it away. She skimmed down her pants and panties at the same time, crouching to slip them off. Then she rose to her height again, totally naked. Heartbreakingly beautiful.

He couldn't stop himself. He reached out.

With a tiny cry, she caught his hand and pressed it flat against the sleek warmth of her belly. "I want…for us to be okay, you know? To work it out. When we got married, the last thing I ever would have imagined was that there could be distance between us. But now…" She let the sentence die unfinished and she looked at him, pleading for reassurance.

Her skin was so silky, her breasts so full and tempting, the nipples puckered, ready for his mouth. And he was so hard it hurt. He would have promised her anything at that moment—the moon, the stars—just to go on touching her, to never have to stop. "We will. We'll be okay."

"I don't know. You say you love me. But you don't seem all that happy about it."

Hadn't they talked enough for now? It damn well seemed like it to him. He turned his hand, captured hers—and pulled her closer. "Kiss me."

She didn't argue, only bent down to him with a small sigh. He breathed in the fresh scent of her. No woman had ever smelled so fine. Their lips met. Hers parted and he tasted her—the heat and the wetness. The sweetness.

No one. Ever, had tasted as good as her.

He needed her closer. He needed to touch her...all over.

Every beautiful, womanly inch of her.

He took her shoulders and pulled her down to him, stretching out with her on the sofa, running his hands over the singing curves of her back, taking the twin globes of her bottom, tucking her into him, hard, rubbing himself against her, letting her feel what she did to him.

She gasped and she whispered his name as she slipped that soft hand of hers between them. Her fingers closed around him.

He thought he would go over the edge, right then and there, though he still had all his clothes on, though all she'd done was to touch him.

It was incredible. Unbearable, what she did to him. He only hoped she would never stop. Slowly, she stroked him, taunting him through the barrier of his clothes.

And when she took his zipper down, he knew he was done for—yet somehow, he held on. He held out, he didn't lose it, as she freed him from the prison of his boxers and his slacks, as she wiggled down his body and took him in her mouth.

He put his hands in her silky hair, clutching her head, looking down at her, amazed at the sight of her soft mouth stretched around him, at the feel of it, so hot and wet, of her naughty tongue rubbing, teasing, all along the length of him.

"I can't," he groaned. "I won't last…"

She went still with a low moan. And then she tipped her head back and looked up at him. Her eyes were full of dreams, her wet mouth so soft. She whispered, "Oh, yeah. You can hold on. And you will…" And she bent her head and claimed him again.

He let out a groan so loud it was close to a shout.

Making little sighing, hungry sounds, she kept on, holding him in place with her hand at the root, working that mouth of hers up and down the shaft….

It was too much.

He was going over.

"No…" He hardly knew how he got the word out. "Not yet. Come up here…" He grabbed her by the shoulders and dragged her, hard, up his body.

"Oh, Brett…" Her eyes were glazed, her ragged breath warm against his face.

He took her mouth in a deep, hungry kiss, groaning his need down low in his throat, spearing his tongue inside, claiming the sweet, slick surfaces beyond her lips, dizzy at the taste of her.

She pushed at his shoulders, urging him to his back. He went, willingly, starved for the feel of her body closing around him. Then she rose up on her knees above him, thighs spread to either side of him—and she lowered her body down onto him, taking him by slow, unbearable degrees.

More low groans escaped him, at the wonder, the glory of it.

Now, he thought in a shattered sort of way. *This. Now…*

No frustration now, no disappointment—in himself, in the way his life, his mind, his body, his heart, all of him lately seemed out of his control.

Now, in the center of this. In the heat and the beauty of it, with his woman above him, her head thrown back, all softness and lush curves, all sweet sighs and hungry cries.

Now, with the feel of her all around him.

It was good. It was right.

"Brett…oh… It's happening…" She said the words and he felt it, too.

Felt her, closing around him, tightening as she reached the peak, her sleek inner muscles contracting around him.

It was too much. It was everything.

His climax caught fire from hers, rolling through him, a ball of flame, searing every nerve as he pushed himself all the way into her.

And she took him. Oh, yeah. She took him.

She was made for him, always had been. Though he'd never known it, for all those years…

His own pulsing started. She cried out loud and collapsed on top of him as the pulsing went on and on. He wrapped his arms tight around her and he emptied himself into her.

It was good.

It was perfect.

He held her close as the fire inside died to a contented glow. Yeah. It was good. For the moment, he felt so sweet and easy.

For the moment, he felt at peace....

Chapter Twelve

Angie sighed and nuzzled Brett's neck. He made a low, rough oh-so-masculine sound that sent a thrill zinging through her, made her clench her inner muscles around him as he slowly softened within her.

He groaned then, and he caught a few strands of her tangled hair between his lips and tugged on them. "You'll kill me."

She said what she always said, "But what a way to go…"

He stroked a teasing finger down her bare arm. "I never even managed to get out of my clothes."

She chuckled. "Sorry. I had to have you. But now I'm somewhat satisfied."

He pressed a kiss against her temple. "Only somewhat?"

"Let me put it this way. If you think I'm done with you, I'm not."

He stroked her hair, smoothing the tangles a little. "Give me a few minutes to recover, before you start making more demands on me."

"I'll try to be patient." She sighed some more and shut her eyes. A little nap, maybe, she thought. Right here, on the sofa, with Brett as her cushion…

He said in a low rumble, "Guess what we forgot?"

"Hmm?"

"Contraception."

She snapped her head up and blinked at him. "Oh, God. You're right…."

He looked more amused than worried. "Chalk up another point for Mother Nature," he said wryly.

She realized she was chewing on her lower lip—and stopped. "I'm sure it'll be all right…."

"Mmm…" He tenderly guided her head back down to the firm pillow of his chest.

"We'll be more careful next time," she vowed.

"Yeah. Absolutely…" He eased his hand up under her hair and rubbed the back of her neck.

She focused on his lovely, slow caresses and tried not to think about what she'd just realized.

Late…

She was late. And the past several days, she'd been suffering from nausea now and then, hadn't she?

But it couldn't be.

No.

She'd been worried, that was all—stressed out over the problems between her and Brett. Over Glory moving away. Stress had made her just a little late.

A voice in her head chided, *Ten days late...*

Her mind skittered away from the scary number. No. Couldn't be...

But she'd been due on the fourth, right? And today was the fourteenth. It was simple subtraction and it came out to...

Ten.

Late, she told herself again. *I'm just real late, that's all....*

Her period would come—that night, or the next day.

No problem. It would be fine...

"Hey," Brett said softly in her ear.

She lifted her head again and they shared a quick kiss. "Umm?"

"What's for dinner?"

She pushed all thoughts of a possible pregnancy from her mind and gave him a big smile. "Baked shells with mozzarella."

He touched the side of her cheek. "Can you hear my stomach growling?"

"Be patient. I have to cook it first." She started to slide off of him.

He wrapped an arm around her and held her there. "Cook it naked."

She put on a stern expression. "Didn't we already discuss the whole 'eating dinner naked' thing?"

"Just while you're cooking, okay? You can get dressed before we eat."

"I don't know. A woman's got to have standards about stuff like this. If I give in on the cooking thing, before you know it, you'll have me at the table, nude."

"You can wear your apron. That frilly one. But nothing else."

"Brett. You have a very naughty mind."

"Yeah. I do. I'm a bad, bad man."

For the next few days, things were better between them. Easier.

And definitely sexier. They made love often.

No, they didn't talk a lot. But Angie told herself to be happy with what she had: a wonderful, smart, sexy husband who loved her to distraction, as she loved him. Meaningful work. Altogether, a good life in a beautiful, light-filled house in her hometown.

Her period didn't come.

She bought a home test when she went down to Grass Valley for groceries Monday, but she didn't take it, though by then she was two weeks late. She stuck the test in the back of a drawer where Brett would never see it and decided to wait just a little bit longer.

Monday night, Glory called.

"Did you tell him you love him?"

"Yeah."

"And…"

"He said he loved me, too—how's New York?"

"New York is just great. My nephew is almost as adorable as Johnny and I signed up for two classes. And don't change the subject."

"I'm not."

"Oh, right. So, he said he loved you, too, and everything's fine at last…."

"It's better."

Glory muttered a bad word. "Okay, so what now?"

"Nothing. I don't know. I miss the way we were, that's all."

"It's those intimacy issues of his, isn't it?"

"Thank you, Dr. Dellazola."

"Go ahead. Be sarcastic—and what else is wrong?"

"What do you mean, what else?"

"I can hear it in your voice. Something else is bothering you."

How did Glory *know* these things? And why weren't they talking about her problems instead of Angie's?

After all, Glory was a single mom struggling to make a place for herself and her baby in the world. She hopelessly loved a violent alcoholic who had left her to sink or swim on her own. Shouldn't *she* be crying on *Angie's* shoulder—instead of the other way around?

"Glory, you should tell me all about your new life. I want to hear everything. I want you to know you can always come to me, to talk, or for whatever you need."

"I do know. And you haven't answered my question. What else is wrong?"

So much for trying to change the subject. Angie gave in and said it out loud for the first time. "I think I'm pregnant."

Dead silence from the other end of the line.

Finally, Angie prompted impatiently, "Hel-lo? You still there?"

"I'm here. Just taking a moment to deal with that one. Since you don't sound the least bit happy, I'm guessing that getting pregnant wasn't in the plan?"

"Of course, it's in the plan. Eventually."

"But…not right now?"

"Well. It's only…we're not ready yet."

"Who ever is?"

"Well, I don't know. But we're not. I mean, we have it all. A nice house, good jobs, a lot in common, great sex. Except for the fact that my husband hates that he's in love with me, everything's perfect."

"Maybe he needs to get counseling."

"Maybe *I* need to get counseling. I need to learn how to be happy with what I've got—and anyway, we agreed to wait a year before we started trying. I went and got a diaphragm, but I don't use it all the time. Sometimes we just get carried away."

"Hey. It happens."

"Then why do I feel like such a cheat?"

"Wait a minute. How 'bout we take this one step at a time? You're *sure* that you're pregnant?"

"Glory, I'm two weeks late."

"You took a test?"

"I bought one—and then I stuck it in the back of a drawer."

"What good's it gonna do you there?"

"Oh, don't start in on me."

"I'm not. I'm tryin' to help. Is Brett there?"

"He's out on a call—why?" Angie asked the question before stopping to think that she didn't really want to hear the answer.

Too late. "Take the test."

"Oh, I don't know…."

"Yeah, you do. Take the test. It *is* one of those ones you can take any time of day, right?"

Oh, she was *so* tempted to lie. "Yeah."

"Take it now. Call me back as soon as you get the results."

"But I…" Angie heard the click from the other end of the line. "Glory? Glory?" Silence, followed by the buzzing of the dial tone. "All right," she grumbled as if Glory could hear her. "Fine. I will. I'll take it right now."

Five minutes later, Angie dialed New York. Glory picked up on the first ring. "Well?"

Angie's throat locked up on her. The best she could manage was a desperate croaking sound. "Argh…Ung…."

"Okay, then. So you *are* pregnant."

Angie set down the test wand with its telltale blue

plus sign in the result window and gulped several times—until her throat loosened up enough that she could talk again. "Uh. Yeah. Yeah, I am."

"And isn't it a relief—to know for sure?"

"Uh…"

"I'll take that as a yes. Now the next step is to tell your husband. Do it right away, as soon as he gets home tonight."

"When did you get so bossy? How did that happen?"

"Angie, tell him. Tonight."

"But—"

"Don't even start. B.J. pulled that on Buck. She waited months to tell him, and all the time, he knew, anyway. Waiting didn't do a thing for either of them— except to make it harder for them to get past all the garbage and get together, where they belong."

Angie tipped her chin high, though her sister wasn't there to see her noble expression. "Look. All I said was—"

"*But,*" Glory finished for her. "You said *but.* It was enough. More than enough. I knew exactly what was comin' next. All about how it's so *early,* all about how you really don't need to talk to Brett about it *yet.* All about how you've got *plenty* of time."

Angie pulled the phone away from her ear long enough to scowl at it. Then she put it back and demanded, "How did you know that?"

"I just told you, it's what B.J. did to Buck. It didn't work for her. And it's not going to work for you, either."

Angie sank into a chair. "It's not?" she asked weakly.

"Think about it. You say you don't feel close to him the way you used to, that he's not *open* with you anymore."

"And it's true. I don't. He's not."

"So you're gonna get him to open up by hiding important information from him?"

"No. I didn't say that. You're twisting what I said."

"Uh-uh, Angie. *You're* the one who's twisting things. You're twisting the truth and wanting honesty and openness from your man."

With a sister like Glory, a girl couldn't get away with anything. "You're boxing me into a corner, you know that?"

"I'm only saying you get what you give."

"All right. I'll tell him."

"Tonight."

"Yeah. Tonight. I promise."

Angie was sitting in the great room with most of the lights on when Brett let himself in the door at eleven-thirty that night. Her heart in her throat, she waited while he hung his jacket on the coatrack and left the open entry area to join her.

"You didn't have to wait up...."

"I wanted to." She marked her place in the book she'd been trying to read and set the book on the side table by her chair. "There's roast chicken...."

He shook his head. "I grabbed a sandwich at the hospital."

She gazed up into his dear face. He looked tired—shadows of fatigue beneath his eyes, the faint lines around his mouth etched a little deeper than usual.

Maybe now wasn't the time. Maybe she should wait until he wasn't quite so tired. Maybe…

No. She cut the excuses off before she could come up with enough of them to convince herself to cop out. Glory was right. It was Brett's baby, too. He should know now.

Her heart knocked against her breastbone and her stomach had suddenly tied itself in a painful clump of knots. "Um, Brett…"

His expression changed. He looked…wary. All of a sudden, there were shadows *in* his eyes as well as under them.

As she watched his guard go up, she had that sense again, strongly. That he didn't really trust her. That he felt he had to protect himself, somehow…protect himself from *her.*

He tried evasion. "Listen, Angie." He actually took a step back from her. "I'm beat. Whatever it is, can it wait until tomorrow?"

Oh, she was doubly tempted then. He didn't want to hear it—and she didn't want to say it. What a pair they were, working so hard, both of them, to keep the things that needed saying from ever getting talked about.

She knew she had to force the damn words out or

he would convince her of what she wanted to believe: that they really didn't need to talk about it now.

"Uh. Nope. Sorry. Can't wait. Really can't. Because, um, well…" She swallowed, convulsively, and pushed the words out. "I'm…pregnant."

Pregnant.

Oh, God. She had said it. She had *told* him.

He fell back another step, and muttered numbly, "You're…?"

She made herself say it again. "I'm pregnant, Brett. I'm two weeks late. And tonight, I took a test. It was positive. We're having a baby."

He ran a hand back over his hair. "Pregnant…" He didn't look mad. But he didn't look particularly happy about it, either.

"I'm sorry." She tugged on the hem of her snug knit shirt, straightening it, just to have something to do with her hands. "I, um, should have been more careful about using my diaphragm. I know you wanted to wait, not to start a family right away. We agreed. That we wouldn't. And really, I wanted to wait, too. But I screwed up." She folded her hands in her lap and looked down at them as she miserably confessed, "Oh, this is awful. I feel like I roped you into this."

"You didn't," he said. She raised her head as he took another step back from her. He was nearly to the fireplace by then. "We'll manage. It will be fine."

She stared at him, achingly aware of the distance he

had just put between them—as he said all the right words, as he promised her that everything was going to be okay.

He was being so understanding. So very kind. Not blaming her. Saying they'd be okay....

But would they, really? How could they? When there was that strange and constant distance between them, when she never really knew what might be going through his mind.

Ask him, she thought. And immediately, a giant wave of hopelessness washed over her. How many times had she asked him? How much good did asking him ever do?

She tried, anyway. "Are you...angry at me? If you are, I'd rather you tell me. I'd rather have it out in the open, where we can talk about it."

"No. I'm not." So calm. So *reasonable.* "You're right. We haven't been...as careful as we should have been. I'm just as much at fault for that as you are. It's not the end of the world, not in the least. We wanted a family, and now we're going to have one."

"Oh, Brett. You make it sound like a punishment."

His brows drew together. "I don't mean it that way."

She shouldn't be so mad at him.

But she was. She was absolutely furious. Her heart beat a swift, angry tattoo and the knots in her stomach had bunched tighter than ever.

She'd messed up and gotten pregnant way ahead of schedule. And now, he was taking it so well, so *reasonably.*

So calmly and logically—and that was a good thing.

Wasn't it?

She knew that it was. And still, she was mad as hell at him. Oh, what was the matter with her?

She strove to keep herself from blurting anything thoughtless, anything that would betray her distinctly *un*reasonable fury. "I don't…I don't know what you *think* anymore. I don't know what you *feel*. It seems like it's all…tangled up, between us—and Brett, that was the thing, you know? It was why I married you. Because we were so *right* with each other. We could tell each other anything, it was all wide open, between us."

"You can still tell me anything." He looked at her dead-on. His eyes gave her nothing and his voice was flat.

"But what about *you*, Brett?" She felt like a living, breathing definition of the word nag. And yet, somehow, she couldn't stop. "Do you think you can tell *me* anything? Because if you do, I'm not getting it, you know? Except when you're making love to me, I don't feel the least bit close to you anymore."

He said nothing for several seconds that seemed like decades. Finally he muttered, "I'm sorry you're upset."

A desperate voice in her head warned, *You've told him you're pregnant. Chalk one up for total honesty. And quit while you're ahead.*

She did nothing of the kind. "You didn't answer my question. Do you still think you can tell me anything?"

Another long silence, then, "Yes."

"I don't believe you."

He shook his head. Slowly. "This is going nowhere. Fast."

She had to agree with him. "I know. You're right. In the past month and a half, it *all* goes nowhere, fast. I ask you, over and over, if something's bothering you. You always say no. There's nothing wrong—and yet, every day you feel farther away from me than the day before. So I…I work up my nerve. I tell you I love you. You say you love me, too. But you're not happy about it. To you, loving me is the worst thing that ever happened to you."

"That is not what I said."

"But it *is* what you meant. Don't try to deny it. You told me you loved me, too. And when I asked you why you never talked to me about anything that matters anymore, you said the state you were in wasn't *conducive* to conversation—and that was all. You wouldn't say any more about it. We made love. It was wonderful. Everything was just fine again. Except it *wasn't* fine. It's *not* fine. It's not fine in the least. It's…it's empty, Brett. It's going through the motions. That's what we do. We go through the motions. Our life is just perfect. Everyone in town envies us. But we don't have what we started out with—at least, I know *I* don't. I had a best friend at the beginning, and I don't anymore. And I want to know, Brett. What in hell have you done with my best friend?"

He didn't answer. What a surprise. He just stared at her, a distant kind of stare that said he didn't want to deal with this—he didn't want to deal with *her.*

Frustrated tears burned in her eyes. One spilled over. She felt it dribble down her cheek as she asked in a whisper, "Why don't you just yell at me? Why don't you just do *something* to let me know you're in there, to let me know you care?"

His lip curled in a sneer. "You'd like that, wouldn't you? If I started yelling at you and carrying on—maybe broke a lamp or two. It would make you feel right at home."

She put a hand to her throat and sucked in a shuddery breath. "Ouch. That hurt."

At least he looked sorry. "You're right. That was out of line—but can't you just be a little patient? Can't you just give it some time? Things will get better, you'll see."

More tears spilled over. "And what if they don't?" She wiped at her damp cheeks, one and then the other, with the back of her hand. "What if we just get farther and farther apart, in our hearts, where it matters? What if you just keep on dragging around here, looking like somebody shot your dog, only coming to life when we're in bed together? I don't know if I can stand that."

"Just wait. You'll see. Things *will* get better." He said the words again—through gritted teeth that time, making her wonder who he was trying so hard to convince.

She argued the obvious. "But things *aren't* getting better. They're getting worse."

He rubbed his eyes, fingers digging into the sockets, then scraped his hands down his weary face. "Angie. Can we just leave it? Can we just…let it be?"

"No. We can't. I'm sorry, but letting it be isn't working for me."

"What do you want me to say?"

"I want to…understand why you're not happy anymore. I want you to explain to me what is going on with you."

He let his arms drop heavily to his sides. "I'm crazy for you, okay? It's…not what I wanted. But it's happened. And now, I'm only waiting for the craziness to pass."

Her frustration rose again. She tried her best to keep it under control, to speak quietly. "Realistically, Brett, what's so horrible about us being in love with each other?"

"It's not what we—"

She threw up both hands. "Okay, okay. It's not what we agreed on, not what we planned. But things could be a whole lot worse—like, say, one of us could have a deadly disease. Or end up in a coma. Or…get burned to a crisp in a flash forest fire. Or, even, say, what if one of us *wasn't* in love with the other? Now, that would be kind of tough. But this? Well, yeah. It was a shock at first, for both of us. But, hey. Try learning to live with it, why don't you? I have. And I've discovered it's just not that much of a hardship to be in love with my own husband!"

"You're shouting," he said darkly.

"You're damn right I am!" she bellowed.

"Bring it down, Angie." He spoke so softly, but the look in his eyes threatened dire consequences if she didn't lower her voice.

Somehow, with great effort, she dialed it down a notch. "The real truth is, I think it's kind of wonderful, really." To that, he made a low, disgusted sort of sound. She resisted the powerful urge to do what she'd sworn she never would: to pick up the nearest lamp and hurl it at his thick Bravo skull. "No, it's not what we planned on. But a lot of the time, life just doesn't go according to plan. It happened. *Love* happened. And instead of dragging around like it's the end of the world, you might just try looking at the problem in a whole new way. You might just try asking yourself what is so terrible about being nuts over your own wife?"

His teeth were clenched so tight, a muscle leaped in his jaw. "The point is, I don't want to be nuts, not even over you. I'm not a nuts kind of guy."

"Brett. Think again. You're nuts for me. You said so yourself. That would make you…a nuts kind of guy."

He shook his head. "It's only temporary. There's solid science on this whole problem and—"

"This problem. The problem of being crazy in love with me?"

"Yeah."

"I'm a problem. I'm your problem."

"That is not what I said."

"Gee. It sure sounded like it. It sounded like you said—"

"Angie. This is going nowhere, degenerating into wild accusations and finger-pointing. I don't want this. I don't want to fight with you."

The irony was, she agreed with him. She always had. Fighting solved nothing. But by then, she just didn't know what else to do. She couldn't bear the thought of going on this way, so far apart, never really talking, until he finally decided he *wasn't* in love with her anymore and let himself be happy again.

She pushed herself out of her chair and held out both hands to him. "Oh, please. Why won't you see? The plans we had when we got married, they didn't work out. *None* of this is turning out the way we planned. We weren't supposed to fall in love. And look at us. We're both completely gone on each other. I wasn't supposed to get pregnant for at least a year. And here I am, having a baby. We weren't going to yell and scream at each other—"

"I have not raised my voice to you."

"Well, whoop-de-do." She lifted a finger and twirled it in the air. "That's just terrific. We're on our way to divorce court, in case you didn't notice. And when we get there, you can tell that to the judge…."

Divorce. Oh, God. Had she really used that word on him? With a shocked cry, she clapped her hand over her mouth.

But it was too late. The D-word hung there, poisoning the air between them. Brett said something not the least reasonable under his breath as they stared at each other, the terrible distance between them yawning wider than ever before.

Into the cavernous silence, Brett asked, "Is that what you want, then, a divorce?"

The softly spoken question shuddered through her like a punch. "No. How can you even think that?"

"Well, Angie. You said it."

"I know. And I shouldn't have." She sank to the chair again, feeling hopeless and miserable and utterly defeated. "But, Brett, I don't know *what* to say to you, how to deal with you, where to…go from here…" She hoped against hope that he would come to her, put a comforting hand on her shoulder, tell her again that it would be all right, even if it wasn't true.

He stayed where he was. "I think enough has been said for one night. More than enough."

If he'd only reach out a hand to her…

But he didn't. And she couldn't blame him. What she'd said was beyond it, dirty fighting in the extreme, exactly the sort of thing they'd always been so certain they'd never pull on each other.

She drew her slumped shoulders back and made herself look at him. "I, um…yeah. We should go to bed, I guess. You go ahead. I'll be there. In a while."

"All right, then."

And that was it. He turned for the bedroom and left her sitting there, thinking how bad she'd messed up, despising herself for letting her temper get the better of her—and still, in her heart, deeply angry with him.

Chapter Thirteen

Angie never joined Brett in their bed that night. She slept in one of the spare rooms.

Brett heard her go down the stairs and thought, Fine. Let her sleep alone.

He was furious at her. Furious, and cut to the core. He didn't dare try to deal with her any more that night. The violence and confusion within him might get loose. He might say or do something from which the two of them as a couple would never recover.

They'd end up yelling at each other. Going at it blow-for-verbal-blow. Living his worst nightmare. Hurting each other beyond the point of saving what they had together, getting completely out of control.

He didn't drop off to sleep until sometime after two.

And when he did, he dreamed of his bad dad, Blake; saw those scary pale gray eyes of his, watching, seeing more than any normal man had a right to see. In the dream, Blake smiled, a psychopath's smile, slow and cruel and deadly. And then he laughed, a laugh like dead leaves rustling in a winter wind, like the dangerous hiss of a poisonous snake.

"No," Brett said. "No…" He looked down to escape the scary pull of those eyes and saw his own hands. A toddler's hands. Small. Dimpled. Weak…

And Blake was towering over him, a dark shadow big enough to block out the sun, to swallow all the light in the world.

Brett woke sitting up, dripping cold sweat, the sheets all tangled around him.

Blinking, arming sweat from his eyes, he saw his own bedroom, the shadowed shapes of bureau and night table, the blue glow of the numbers on the digital clock. Beyond the window, through the dark, rising from the steep bank across the river, the tall pines loomed into the star-thick mountain sky.

Angie's side of the bed was still empty.

Probably just as well.

He got up, went to the bathroom, drank water from the tap and took special care not to meet his own eyes in the wide mirror that spanned the long counter and the two sinks. Back in the bedroom, he straightened the covers and got into bed again, turning on his side, away from the empty place where his wife should have been.

The next morning they were elaborately careful with each other—polite and mostly silent. That was fine with Brett. They went to the clinic…and they got through the day by keeping it strictly professional, both of them focusing all their attention right where it was supposed to be: on caring for their patients.

At home that evening, Angie cooked dinner while Brett sat in his favorite easy chair in the living room reading the *Sacramento Bee*. When the food was ready, they ate in the breakfast nook, a silent meal, one during which they both carefully avoided making eye contact.

Glory called at seven. Angie took the call downstairs. A half an hour later, she came back up, her eyes and nose red and puffy. Though she pointedly did *not* speak to him or look his way, Brett got the message loud and clear. She'd been crying on the phone to her baby sister.

He probably shouldn't have let that get to him, shouldn't begrudge her someone to talk to when she was feeling low. But he did begrudge her. He felt betrayed. He wondered what kind of rotten stuff she'd been saying to Glory about him.

But he didn't ask. He didn't say a damn word.

There was no sense in going there. Nothing but trouble would come of it.

She disappeared into their bedroom. He stared blankly at the TV, but he couldn't keep himself from glancing up when she emerged a few minutes later with her tooth-paste, toothbrush, that special soap she used and what looked like a pair of lightweight pajamas—though he couldn't be sure if the wad of yellow cloth was pajamas or not. She'd never worn pajamas in their bed....

He forced himself to stare at the TV again, to watch Keith Oberman's lips move, to ignore the bleak sound of her footsteps moving away from him, going back down the stairs.

By the next night, Wednesday, when he got home late from the hospital in Grass Valley and found their bed empty again, he realized that this stand-off was getting to be a pattern; they were leading separate lives under the same roof.

He knew he should do something about it. But he was still so damn mad at her. He was afraid of the things he might say if he marched down the stairs, rousted her from the bed in the spare room and tried to talk to her.

So he put it off.

Later, he thought—when he didn't want to grab her and shake her until she came to her senses and started acting rationally. When he didn't want to shout at her so bad it made an itching sensation under his skin.

Thursday went by in pretty much the same way as the days before it. Friday, as well.

Saturday, she ran the vacuum and washed windows

in the morning. He went over to the clinic to catch up on some paperwork. When he got back at noon, she wasn't there.

But she'd left a note on the table. *Having lunch at the diner. Going swimming after. Back by four. Dinner at my parents'. Six o'clock.*

Right, he thought. It was Dani's birthday, wasn't it? Angie had mentioned the party last week.

Back when they were still speaking to each other.

Still *sleeping* with each other…

And who the hell was she having lunch with, anyway?

Not that it mattered. Not that he needed to know…

When they got to the Dellazola house that night, Angie went straight to the kitchen to join the women. Brett took a chair in the family room with the men, who were watching a wrestling match on Little Tony's bigscreen TV. No one seemed to notice that Angie and her husband weren't getting along.

At seven-fifteen, Rose called everyone to the table. They all got up and headed for the dining room—and Trista started screaming.

Little Steffie had vanished again.

The frantic search began. Since they were all running up and down the stairs, several of them in every room, Brett headed for the front door—which he found, mysteriously, slightly ajar.

Steffie wasn't on the front porch. He hurried down

the steps and across the lawn—and spotted her shining brown hair as she toddled off down Jewel Street.

"Steffie!" He shouted and took off at a run.

The kid stopped and turned. He saw her smile. "Docca Bwett!" she called.

He caught up with her quickly and scooped her into his arms. She hugged him and patted the back of his neck with her soft little hand. "I go for a walk," she proudly announced when she pulled back to grin at him again.

"You should ask your mommy first."

She pinched up her tiny mouth. "Oops."

He carried her quickly back to the brick steps and up them as the Dellazolas emerged in a pack from the house, every one of them shouting.

"There she is!"

"Brett's got her!"

"Well, wouldn't you know?"

The family surrounded them, laughing, joking how they all knew he'd be the one to save the day. He passed the little girl to her sobbing mother.

Rose said, "Oh, Brett. How did we ever get along without you?"

He muttered something appropriately modest and low-key—and scanned the crowd around him, seeking Angie.

She was there, but standing back on the porch steps. When he tried to catch her eye, her gaze slid away.

They couldn't continue like this and he knew it.

That night, when they got home, they were talking this out.

A half hour later, after Old Tony offered a long-winded toast to Dani, the birthday girl, Ike tapped his glass with his butter knife and stood.

"Ahem. To my beautiful wife. Happy birthday, my darlin'." He waited for everyone to raise their glasses and drink, before adding, "And, Dani has news." He beamed at his wife. "The *best* news."

"Oh, yes." Dani's eyes shone with happy tears. "The best birthday present ever…"

Rose let out a cry. "A baby? A little one? You two are giving me a grandchild, at last?"

Dani and Ike bobbed their heads in unison and everyone at the table erupted into clapping and cheering and shouts of "Congratulations!" Angie, Trista and Clarice all jumped up in unison and ran to Dani, surrounding her, all of them hugging her at once.

Brett clapped his hands like everyone else and watched his wife hugging her sister and couldn't help thinking about the baby he and Angie would have.

It wouldn't have been the right time, and Brett knew it, for him and Angie to announce that they were having a baby, too.

No. This was Dani's and Ike's moment. They'd waited a long time for this. And it was Dani's day, anyway.

It would have been good, though, to have Angie at least glance his way, meet his eyes, to share a secret smile in honor of their own baby, the one they'd be announcing to the family in the next month or two....

He was happy about the baby, he truly was, now that he'd had a few days to deal with the fact that baby was coming.

He knew he needed to tell Angie that.

And he would, damn it. Tonight. When they got home...

The evening wore on. Angie granted him no glances—let alone any smiles.

And as the hours went by and she wouldn't even look at him, he started remembering all the reasons he was mad at her. He kept hearing her voice, making that rotten crack about how they would end up in divorce court, kept thinking of the way she'd yelled at him, of how she demanded that he be happy over feeling things he damn well didn't want to feel.

Aunt Stella took him aside as the party broke up. "Don't forget..."

"I know, Stella. Angie needs to go see Father Delahunty."

"I don't know what's wrong with her. It's an important step. I can't see why she won't take it."

Because she thinks we're going to end up divorced, anyway, he thought. He said, "I'll talk to her. Again."

"Good. You keep after her. See she does what's right."

Great idea. He'd be sure to talk to her about it. If he ever talked to her again.

At home, Angie went downstairs and he went to the master suite.

Sunday dragged by. And Monday and Tuesday. Over a week since she'd moved into the room downstairs.

And still, they went on. Living like strangers in the same house.

Wednesday started out the same. A silent breakfast, a morning at the clinic where they kept it to the week-long pattern of brisk, impersonal professionalism. At lunchtime, she told him she was taking the rest of the day off. She said she had a few errands to run.

Fine with him. Things weren't all that busy. He could keep up with the patient load on his own. And it was just easier, without her around, without that constant undercurrent of angry tension between them.

He got home at five-thirty and found her matching set of blue suitcases waiting at the door. She rose from a chair by the fireplace and came toward him.

"What the hell?" he said.

She stopped about three feet from him, arms at her sides, shoulders back, head high—and eyes moist with unshed tears. "I need some time away, Brett. This whole thing, here with you…" She paused to clear her throat before going on. "It's not working. I feel awful all the time."

Tell her you need to talk. Go ahead. Say it. But somehow, he couldn't. "And you think you'll feel better if you move out on me?"

She cast a put-upon glance at the ceiling—as if

there might be answers up there. Then she wiped at her eyes, cleared her throat a second time and said, "I don't know if I'll feel better. But I'm pretty darn sure I can't feel any worse."

Talk to me, Angie. Please. "Where will you go?"

"Where else? My mother's. They're not going to be happy to see me, I know it. But I'll deal with that when I get there."

"They don't know you're coming?"

"They will in a few minutes."

He pictured them all—her mom, her aunt, Old Tony—shouting at her, telling her what a total fool she was to have left him. He realized he couldn't stand the thought of all of them getting on her. Even if they were telling her what he wanted her to hear.

She looked…tired. And kind of pale.

Funny, he'd been so busy the last week trying not to meet her eyes, he hadn't really looked at her. "Angie. Are you ill?"

She gave a tight shrug. "Morning sickness and too much stress, that's all. I'll be okay…" She didn't say it, but the rest was there in her tear-filled eyes: she'd be okay, once she got away from him.

"Angie…" Damn. How to start? What to say? He had no idea how to even begin…

How had they come to this?

Now, when it was probably too late, he felt a grudging admiration for all the times she'd gutted it up and tried to bridge the growing gap between them.

"It only seemed right," she said, "to tell you to your face that I was leaving. So I waited until you got home."

"Angie..."

"Goodbye, Brett."

He caught her arm as she moved to go around him. "Wait."

She looked down at his hand gripping her elbow and then back up at him. A single tear rolled a shining path down her soft cheek. "Let go of me. Please."

Somehow, he made himself release her and then he told her flatly, "You're going nowhere."

She stepped back, her pale face flushing, her mouth drawn tight. "You think you can keep me here? Think again."

"I'll go."

She gaped. "You'll...what?"

"I'll go. You stay here."

"But that's not right."

"Of course it is."

"Brett. It's your house."

"It's *our* house. And you're not leaving it."

"I couldn't do that, kick you out."

"You're not. I'm volunteering. You need some time away from me, fine. You stay. I'll go."

"Oh, Brett..." She shut her eyes. When she finally looked at him again, she asked in a whisper, "Where would you go?"

"The Sierra Star. You know Ma. She's great. Minds

her own business." He didn't say, "unlike *your* family."
But he didn't need to say it.

She wiped more tears away. "You're sure?" He
could hear the relief in her voice—that she wouldn't
have to throw herself on the mercy of her family, who
would all rally 'round, to love her and take care of
her—and never shut up until she did things their way.

He nodded. "Give me ten minutes to get my stuff
together and I'm out of here."

Chapter Fourteen

The next evening, when Angie got home, alone, from the clinic at five-fifteen, the phone was ringing. She rushed to answer—and almost wished she hadn't.

It was her mother. "Angela Marie, are you crazy?"

The gossip mill had ground slowly this time. It had taken a full twenty-four hours for word of Brett's moving out to reach her family. "Uh, no, Mamma. I've got all my marbles *and* the bag I keep them in."

"Don't talk back to your mother," Aunt Stella said tightly from the other extension.

In the background, her great-grandfather hollered, "Angie, what's happened to you? You were always a good girl!"

"It's all over town that you kicked Dr. Brett out of his own house," her mother accused. "Oh, Angie. What, by all the saints, is the matter with you?"

"A wife's sacred duty is to cleave to her husband," Aunt Stella intoned.

"Angie!" Old Tony yelled. "Call your husband! Beg him to come home to you!"

"A good man," said her mother. "A *great* man. Your husband is the best there is and—"

"Mamma."

"You were always so happy together."

"Mamma."

"I just can't believe that you've—"

"Mamma!"

A blessed silence on the line, followed by a thoroughly exasperated, "What?"

"If you're going to call me up just to yell at me, I'm not going to take your calls."

Aunt Stella gasped. Loudly. "Well, I never…"

Old Tony yelled something really rude in Italian. "Angie, you go to your husband. Get down on your—"

"I mean it, Mamma. And that goes for Grandpa Tony, too."

"Just a minute," said her mother tartly. The line went mute. Seconds later, her mother spoke again. "Okay. They're gone."

"Aunt Stella?"

"Both of them. I promise you." Her mother's voice was softer now. "I'm sorry, Angela." She was honestly contrite. "You know how we are. We love you. We want what's best for you. And sometimes we get carried away."

Angie answered gently. "I know, Mamma. It's okay."

"You and Brett, you'll…work this out?"

"I hope so…" She felt the tears rising. Again. Lately she was a human waterworks. Her marriage was on the rocks. And she was pregnant. Misery and raging hormones: not a good combination.

"Oh, Angie…"

"Mamma, I can't talk now." Angrily, she dashed the first tears away. There were more coming. She wouldn't be able to hold them back for long. "I have to go. I'm sorry…."

"You should have someone to tell your troubles to."

"I've got Glory."

"Good. And remember. Anytime you need me, I'm here."

"Thanks, Mamma. Gotta go…"

Angie hung up as the tears got away from her and flowed down her cheeks. No, a crying jag never solved anything. But right then, she couldn't stop herself. It all seemed so sad and hopeless, an endless tunnel of misery, with no light in sight. She dropped to the break-fast nook table and put her head in her hands.

After five minutes of hard sobbing, she blew her nose and dried her eyes and got up to see about dinner. She might be a crying fool who couldn't make her marriage work, but for the sake of her unborn baby, she would damn well eat right.

As she got the ingredients together for meat loaf, she couldn't help wondering, What would Brett do for dinner? Maybe Chastity would cook for him. Or he'd head over to the Nugget, sit alone in the booth they used to share…

He'd looked really tired, today, at the clinic.

She hoped he was okay. She missed him. So much.

But that was nothing new, really.

She'd been missing him for months. The only difference now was that he was actually gone….

Nadine plunked Brett's dinner in front of him.

He picked up his steak knife. "'Nother whiskey."

"Not that it's any of my business, but that will be your third."

"You're right. It's none of your business. Bring me another drink."

"What if you get an emergency call?"

Brett looked down at his steak and then up again at Nadine, who stood over him, showing no inclination to give it up and go away. Whatever happened to the good old days? he wondered. Back when waitresses did what a man told them to do. "Fine, Nadine. *Don't* bring me that drink. Just go away. Let me eat my steak in peace."

She muttered something that sounded suspiciously like, *Somebody needs to go back to his wife.*

"Go. Now."

"Don't point that steak knife at me," she growled. But at least, when she finished grumbling, she left.

Brett ate. He left the money on the table, including a much larger tip than an interfering waitress such as Nadine deserved. He yearned to go over to the St. Thomas and get seriously snockered.

But he didn't. Because Nadine was right. He might get a call and he'd never forgive himself for crapping out when a patient needed him.

He went back to the Sierra Star and spent the rest of the night wishing Angie would call—and not quite managing to pick up the phone and call *her*.

On Friday, at the clinic, he dared to ask his estranged wife how she was feeling.

"I'm okay."

"If you need anything…"

"No, really, Brett. I'm fine." And she headed for the nearest exam room to give an injection.

He stared after her, thinking this had to stop. They needed to work things out.

But they didn't. They went on in the same way: she in the house, he at the B and B. Through that night. And Saturday.

Everyone in town was talking. Some, like Nadine, even said things in front of him. Since nobody knew what was really going on, they made things up. A number of wild stories circulated: that Brett had another woman. That Angie had another guy. That she wanted to leave town and he didn't. That he was sick and tired of her interfering family and had told her to make a choice—the Dellazolas or him.

He didn't let the talk bother him—well, okay. The one about Angie having someone else kind of got to him. But since he knew it wasn't true, he could ignore it. He'd lived in the Flat long enough to be pretty good at tuning out the gossip mill.

Sunday he woke to buttery-yellow sunlight pouring in the window of his charming rented room and he didn't even want to get out of the damn bed. Why get up? Ahead lay a grim stretch of hours to be faced and waded through.

By nine, lying there doing nothing seemed even worse than getting up and going through the motions of living his life. He showered. Shaved. Hustled downstairs to get some breakfast.

He was the only one in the dining room. The current group of guests were all early risers. His mother poured his coffee, served him his eggs Benedict and a basket of muffins. He picked up the *Bee* and was just reading the headlines on the front page, when Chastity reappeared. He saw her from the corner of his eye as she came in from the kitchen. She marched over to him, hauled back a chair and sat down in it—hard.

Slowly he lowered his paper. "What's the matter, Ma?"

"You," she said. "You're makin' me sick."

Crap. He didn't need this—and from Chastity, of all people. One of his mother's most admirable qualities was how she knew enough to stay out of what didn't concern her. "Back off," he said gently. And raised his paper again.

That was when she grabbed it from his hands, wadded it up and threw it at the sideboard. "Come in the kitchen. I got things to say to you."

Sunday, Angie went to early mass. Her mom was there—and Tris, Clarice and Dani, and Aunt Stella, too. They all sat together.

Afterwards, no one said a word about how Angie had stayed in the pew while the rest of them took communion. Angie appreciated that they kept their mouths shut. Her mom urged her to come up to the house. Angie shook her head and said she had a lot to do at home. It was true. She had the dusting. And she was slowly working her way through the endless big windows upstairs and down, giving each one a good cleaning.

And then, in the afternoon, she was thinking that maybe she'd go down to Grass Valley and catch a movie. Really, her life was just packed—in a sad and lonely sort of way. She hugged them all: her mom and aunt and sisters. And then she waved goodbye and walked home through the warm, bright morning to the house by the river.

She made herself breakfast and then cleaned up after, wiping all the counters thoroughly, until they shone. She tackled the dusting.

Okay, it was kind of pitiful. All this cleaning. But while she cleaned, she could think.

About what to do next. About how to break this awful stalemate between herself and the man she loved.

The thing was, she still felt that she'd done all she could. That he, finally, had to come to her, meet her halfway. Or it was no good.

At least, she felt that way half the time.

The other half, she blamed herself for causing so much trouble, for demanding things of Brett he just didn't seem to be capable of giving. Then, all she knew was that she was hurting and hurting bad—that he was hurting, too.

That she needed to patch things up, to take what he was willing to give of himself, to learn to be happy with what she had.

Windows next. She got her squeegee and her extension pole and she mixed up a bucket of cleaning solution. Outside on the deck, she hosed off a tall window and started in, sponge side first, going through the motions of the job by rote, her mind on Brett, on how much she missed him, how she couldn't stand being away from him, wanted to work things out with him....

She had no idea she wasn't alone until a hulking figure loomed behind her, reflected darkly in the window glass, and a rough voice, a voice from her worst real-life nightmare, said much too quietly, "Hey, babe. Lookin' good."

Jody.

Angie froze, arm extended, the squeegee high against the window. Her mouth went all coppery, her stomach rolled and the muscles on the back of her neck twitched and knotted. Cold sweat broke out on her upper lip. She clutched the extension pole in a stranglehold. If she turned fast enough, if she hit him with the pole…

"Don't even think about it." He laughed, a low, mean sound that scraped along her nerves like a shard of broken glass. "No sudden moves, now. You and me, we need to talk." She felt the cold kiss of something metal at the small of her back—a gun. Oh, sweet Lord. He had a gun. "Drop the pole." He dug that gun into her spine. "Now."

She let it go. It bounced on the end of the handle and then slowly tipped over, clattering down, the squeegee end landing across the railing, at a forty-five degree angle. It rolled back and forth and then stopped, the handle on the deck, the other end sticking out over the railing.

"Good," Jody said. "Now turn around, baby. Turn around real slow."

Chapter Fifteen

Against his own better judgment, Brett rose and followed his mother as she headed for the kitchen.

Once they got there, she shut the door and flung out a hand in the direction of the table. "Sit," she commanded, as if he was an ill-behaved dog.

Really, she was kind of scaring him. Acting so unlike herself, all het up and ready to kick some serious butt—his, apparently.

He sat. "Okay. What? Spit it out."

She did, in a rush of angry words. "You are too damn proud, Brett Bravo. Too proud for you own good. And I've always worried for you—and for Brand. I worry for you two more than I ever did for Buck or even

Bowie. Buck and Bowie, they get it right out there. They're not afraid to love with all their crazy hearts. They mess up and mess up bad, but they keep goin'. They keep trying. You and Brand, you hold yourselves away from life—and from love. You took a lesson from your awful daddy, from my pitiful refusal to see him as he really was. It wasn't a good lesson. You think love—real love, true love—is a bad thing. You fear it, you fear it deep down in your soul. You hide from it— Brand, from his love for Charlene. You, from lovin' that sweet wife of yours the way she deserves to be loved."

He opened his mouth to deny what she said.

She cut him off before he could get a word out. "No," she commanded. "Wait. Don't you start spouting any scientific mumbojumbo at me. Don't you use that big brain of yours on me to shut me up. You hear me out." She glared, daring him to interrupt. He didn't. She continued. "I was so happy, when you finally admitted that Angie was the one for you, when you two ran off and got married. I actually believed you'd figured it out— gotten past your own fear of loving, of trusting. That at last you understood. It was never lovin' itself that was to blame. It's *who* you love that matters, that you have the sense to choose a worthy heart to give your love to. I chose wrong. And then, for too many years, I refused to see my choice for the disaster it was. I was a bad mother. And for that, my children have had to pay."

In spite of the way the things she said made his gut churn and his blood run hot and fast, she *was* his mother. And she'd done her best. He jumped to her defense. "Ma, don't say that. You did okay. You——"

She silenced him with her strong hand on his shoulder, her fingers digging in. "No. Don't make excuses for me. I don't want them. Or need them. What I want is for you to stop being so afraid of loving Angie. What I want is for you to go to her and tell her you're ready to stand up beside her, you're ready to stop running away from the love that you have for her."

The denials rose up in him again. But this time, he swallowed them down.

Damn it. She was right.

His mother had him pegged.

Funny, but as soon as he admitted that, the knot in his stomach eased and his racing heartbeat slowed.

He hung his head and confessed, "I've been telling myself it would run its course, that it was only a biological urge, that all I had to do was wait it out."

Chastity made a snorting sound. "I loved your father for thirty years. Are you prepared to wait that long, to make yourself and Angie miserable for three decades—or more?"

He swore. It was one of those words a man shouldn't say in front of his mother. Then he lifted his head and looked up at her. "I guess I've really screwed up, huh?"

Her smile had all the wisdom of the world in it. "You're lucky that wife of yours loves you so much. I'll bet she's just waitin' for you to come to your senses."

"God. I hope you're right."

She squeezed his shoulder again. "Go on, now. Don't hang around here a minute longer. You go to her. You *make* it right."

He decided he'd walk over.

It was a gorgeous day, a great day to be on foot. Plus, the walk would take six or seven minutes—as opposed to three in the SUV. He could use the time to figure out how to tell Angie what a hopeless fool he'd been.

Was he stalling?

Yeah, well. Maybe a little. But what the hell difference would three minutes make?

He started off down the street, walking briskly, rehearsing the things he would say to her, telling himself she'd forgive him for the living hell he'd put her through the past several weeks, hoping against hope that he was right. Folks waved as he went by them. He waved back, hardly seeing them, his mind on Angie, on how he was going to make things right.

In no time at all, he was turning onto Catalpa Way, walking fast, approaching the house, the moment of truth almost upon him.

Strange. All the blinds were drawn…

At ten in the morning?

That didn't make sense. Angie was an early riser. She was always up by seven and the first thing she would do in the morning was to open all the blinds for the day.

His steps slowed as he came even with the house, on his way to the driveway on the south side. He spotted that squeegee she used on the windows, fallen half over the railing, as if she'd dropped it and just left it there. That big pink bucket of hers waited, too, beneath a streaked-looking window.

Shivers of apprehension crawled beneath his skin. It didn't add up, her washing windows with the blinds shut.

And she was such a tidy kind of person. She wouldn't walk off and leave her equipment hanging halfway off the deck.

Brett picked up his pace again—but now he was careful, to tread lightly, to make as little sound as possible as he rounded the side of the house and moved close to it, heading up the bank beside it.

Okay, he was probably overreacting. It was probably nothing—the drawn blinds, the abandoned bucket and pole. But some deeper instinct had kicked in. If there *was* trouble inside the house, he wanted to get the jump on it, to assess the situation before he revealed his presence.

He scaled the steep bank, watching where he put his feet, taking care not to dislodge any rocks or gravel. The shades were drawn everywhere he looked, including the side window at the lower floor. The window itself was shut. As he came even with it, he pressed his ear to it, but heard no sounds within.

On this side, at the upper level, only the four-inch-thick glass-block bathroom window was near the bank. No sense trying to hear anything through that.

He reached the concrete retaining wall that jutted off the entrance side of the house. Lightly, he hoisted himself onto it—and over the decorative split-rail fence that ran between the house and the garage. He hustled up the front walk—and found what he was looking for. One of the breakfast nook windows was raised.

Through the screen and the drawn blinds, faintly, he heard a voice from inside. It was deep and rough. Clearly male.

He crept to the window and listened.

"The money," the voice said. "Now."

"Jody…" That was Angie's voice, low and even, carefully controlled. But he could hear the terror in it. And the hatred, too. If Brett had ever been jealous of the bastard who hurt her, he never would be again. "I've only got about a hundred in cash," she said.

"Get it. And your checkbook and credit cards, too."

"If you'd only—"

"Shut up."

"But—"

"You think I won't shoot you, bitch?"

Not good, Brett thought. Not good at all. Jody had a gun. That would make things harder.

The crook demanded, "The money. Where?"

"My purse. On the kitchen counter."

"Let's go. Over there. Now."

Brett heard the footsteps coming toward the kitchen and had to accept that the open window wasn't going to do it for him. The S.O.B. would shoot him before he got the damn screen off. A pity, too, because Brett owned a nice pair of hunting rifles. He kept them safely hidden in a special panel built into the kitchen ceiling.

No way he could get to them, though. He'd have to improvise some kind of weapon—but first, he had to get inside the house.

Brett turned back the way he had come. Moving swiftly on silent feet, he went over the rail fence and ran full-out down the bank to the patio below, chancing a minor slide that might have been heard inside.

The French door to the central downstairs room was locked. But he had his key. Too bad he didn't have a cell phone, damn it. He could call 9-1-1, get the sheriff over here.

But cell phones didn't work in the Flat. The surrounding mountains cut off the signals. He was on his own.

He let himself in, shut the door with aching, silent care and took off his shoes.

Now, for a weapon.

The door to the spare room that they'd been using for storage stood ajar. He went to it, slipped inside. A sturdy-looking handle stuck out of a box of kitchen stuff that Angie had brought from the cottage: a cast-iron frying pan.

It wasn't a rifle. But if he could get the jump on Jody and swing it good and hard, it would deliver one hell of a blow.

Frying pan in hand, Brett soundlessly opened the

door again and crept toward the stairwell. He could hear the scumball talking upstairs, giving Angie orders. "Over there. Sit down." A silence, as Brett moved up the stairs—and, presumably, Angie did what the dirtbag told her to do. Then he was yakking again. "Nice setup you got here. I like me a woman who lands on her feet. I heard all about you. Piece of cake, gettin' all the news I needed. Lotsa people in this town with real big mouths. Hear you're havin' a few problems with that new husband of yours—real sad, Angie baby. You got such bad luck with men…"

A low wall rimmed the stairwell. Brett crouched as he reached the top step. Carefully, he peered around the wall.

And got lucky.

Angie sat in a chair, facing Brett. Jody stood over her, pistol in one hand, Angie's wallet and checkbook in the other, talking a mile a minute. "Now, the big question, Angie, honey, is what am I gonna to do with you? I got me some trouble, you know? Big trouble…"

Brett emerged from the stairwell. Angie saw him—and somehow, amazingly, managed not to give him away. Her gaze stayed flat, wary. It showed no surprise, only carefully controlled fear of the muscle-bound crook in dirty jeans and a torn T-shirt who loomed over her. She had a bruise on her cheekbone, blood in the corner of her mouth.

Brett knew rage then, a boiling fury—icy at the same time as it burned. The bastard had hit her, *hurt* her. Again.

He made himself breathe slow and even. Above all, from here on, he mustn't lose focus. He had one solid chance—maybe. If he worked it right, he might get in one good blow. If he screwed up, Jody would shoot him.

Jody kept on talking. "I'm thinkin' I'm better off to leave no witnesses, babe." Brett moved forward, on the balls of his feet, making no sound. Jody said, "I'm thinkin', if you can't talk, who's gonna know it was me that was here to see you?"

"Well, Jody…" She dared to speak up, though he'd ordered her not to. Brett knew why. She wanted to make sure the guy's attention didn't wander, that he didn't just happen to glance over his shoulder. "People *would* know," she said. "The people you talked to in town, the people who told you all about me, remember?"

Jody muttered an obscenity. "You think you're so damn smart. You always did. And you never did listen when I told you to keep that trap of yours shut." He hauled back his gun hand to hit her again.

Brett was in place by then, not two feet away. He raised the frying pan high and brought it down on the back of Jody's head. It made a weird bonging sound. The shock of the blow jittered up Brett's arms.

Angie gasped and brought her hand to her mouth.

And Jody Sykes dropped like a sack of rocks.

Chapter Sixteen

Angie called for help.

In ten minutes, the sheriff was there. Jody was still out cold when the EMTs appeared two minutes after that. He started groaning as they examined him.

Brett let the med techs deal with him. They checked his vitals and loaded him onto a gurney. He was semiconscious by then, muttering under his breath, disconnected phrases, as they carried him out.

In Brett's professional opinion, he was a prime candidate for a deadly case of post-concussive syndrome.

The sheriff took them—Angie first, Brett second—into one of the empty rooms downstairs. They each gave their story. The tech guy came and took pictures—

of the spot on the rug where Jody had bled, of the frying pan and the checkbook and wallet, of the "scene of the incident" from a number of angles.

They bagged and tagged. And finally, about three hours after Brett bopped Jody with the pan, they had what they needed and were ready to leave.

As he was going out the door, the sheriff paused to confide, "Don't worry, Brett. We got a lot on Jody Sykes—and that's besides what he did here today, and to Angie in San Francisco."

"He might not pull out of it," Brett said with real regret. If he had it to do over again, he would. In a minute. But still, he *was* a doctor. His job was to heal, not kill.

The sheriff gave him a bleak grin. "Don't worry. We'll see he gets the best medical care there is—and then we'll put him away for forty years."

The sheriff's SUV was barely down the driveway before Angie's mom and dad—followed by Chastity in her old pickup—came driving up. Word had already spread around town that Angie had been attacked and Brett had saved the day.

There was much crying and hugging. Rose fussed over the bruise on Angie's cheek and called Brett a hero—again. Little Tony put his arm around him and called him, "Son."

Brett grabbed Chastity and squeezed her good and hard. "Thanks, Ma."

She laid her hand on his cheek. "Looks like I set you straight just in time."

Angie made coffee and offered a late lunch. Of course, everybody stayed.

It was four in the afternoon before Brett and his wife were finally alone. He shut the door and locked it.

And then he took her in his arms.

With a tender sigh, she rested her head against his shoulder. "Oh, I have missed you. I'm so glad you're home."

"I've been a first-class jerk. Not to mention, a fool."

"Yeah. Yeah, you have. But I'm so happy that you're *my* fool…." She lifted her mouth to him. And he took it in a slow, deep, hungry, kiss.

When he raised his head and she gazed up at him, eyes shining, that dimple he adored showing in her cheek, he said, "I love you, Angie. I'm *in love* with you. I plan to stay that way. For the rest of our lives."

She kissed his chin. "You think maybe you could get used to it, then, to loving me? Is that what you're telling me?"

"I'm telling you I know I can trust you. I'm telling you that it's an honor, to be in love with you."

"Oh, Brett." She cuddled into his shoulder again. "It's nice…to hear the words."

He nuzzled her hair. "Well, you've been saying for a long time now that I don't talk to you anymore."

"Yeah. But it's funny…"

"What?" he demanded gruffly.

"When you came up the stairs with that old frying pan in your hand, somehow I knew…"

He teased, "That Jody Sykes was going down?"

"Oh, yeah. There was that—and it was a big relief, I can tell you. But I also knew…that it would be okay, between us. That we would be really *together* again."

"All that in an instant?"

She laughed. "That's right. And now, well, the words are nice. But it's looking in those eyes of yours and knowing that you're really *here,* with me. That you love me and you know it, that you're mine and I'm yours… That's it. That's the bottom line. Everything else is just gravy, you know?"

He did know. So he kissed her again.

And again, after that.

And then he swept her high in his arms and carried her to the bed where he'd been so lonely without her.

They made slow, sweet love, in the dim, early evening light that peeked in through the tilted slats of the blinds.

Later, he told her how much he wanted the baby. "It's earlier than we planned, I know, but a baby is just fine. A baby is great. Please believe me."

"Oh, Brett. I do believe you. I don't doubt you now. I can see the truth, shining there in your eyes."

"And tomorrow, no matter what, you'll go and see Father Delahunty, arrange to do whatever we have to do, so we'll be married in the eyes of your church."

"I will. First thing. Oh, Brett. It's a promise…"

Epilogue

Six months later, Angie and Brett stood before Father Delahunty in the New Bethlehem Flat Catholic Church. Outside, a light snow drifted down to cover the ground in a blanket of purest white. In the front pew on the bride's side, Mamma Rose was sobbing and Aunt Stella was sniffling.

Father Delahunty asked, "Have you come here freely and without reservation to give yourselves, each to the other, in holy matrimony?"

Angie had eyes only for Brett as they answered, together, "We have."

"Will you love and honor each other as husband and wife for as long as you both shall live?"

They replied, "We will."

"Will you accept children lovingly from God and bring them up according to the law of Christ and his Church?" In the second-row pew, Trista was heard to clear her throat at that one.

Angie only smiled, put her hand on the ripe bulge of her tummy and, in unison with her soon-to-be husband, proudly declared, "We will."

Father Delahunty invited them to exchange their vows.

Angie said hers softly, repeating the age-old promise with slow and tender care.

Brett's deep voice was firm and sure when he gave the sacred words back to her.

"I, Brett, take you, Angela, for my lawful wife, to have and to hold from this day forward, for better, for worse, for richer, for poorer, in sickness and in health, for all the days of my life."

From this day forward...

The solemn words echoed in Angie's mind and heart, during the blessing of the rings, the offering of prayers, the "Our Father" and the final nuptial blessing.

Father Delahunty gave the sign of peace, offered a last prayer and then announced to all present, "Mr. and Mrs. Brett Bravo."

In the front pew, Angie's mother sobbed a little louder than before. Glory, who'd come all the way from New York for this special day, beamed wide.

Angie went into her husband's open arms. He kissed

her and when he did, whispered, "From this day forward…" as if he had known what she was thinking, known exactly what was in her heart.

She smiled against his lips, thinking, *Well, of course he knows.*

He always had.

He was her husband. Her best friend. Her companion. The man who owned her heart, and thrilled her with just a touch.

She was his and he was hers.

For all the days of their lives.

* * * * *

Set in darkness beyond the ordinary world.
Passionate tales of life and death.
With characters' lives ruled by laws the everyday
world can't begin to imagine.

Introducing NOCTURNE, a spine-tingling new line
from Silhouette Books.

The thrills and chills begin with UNFORGIVEN by
Lindsay McKenna.

Plucked from the depths of hell, former military sharp-shooter Reno Manchahi was hired by the government to kill a thief, but he had a mission of his own. Descended from a family of shape-shifters, Reno vowed to get the revenge he'd thirsted for all these years. But his mission went awry when his target turned out to be a powerful seductress, Magdalena Calen Hernandez, who risked everything to battle a potent evil. Suddenly, Reno had to transform himself into a true hero and fight the enemy that threatened them all. He had to become a Warrior for the Light....

Turn the page for a sneak preview of UNFORGIVEN
by Lindsay McKenna.
On sale September 26, wherever books are sold.

Chapter 1

One shot...one kill.

The sixteen-pound sledgehammer came down with such fierce power that the granite boulder shattered instantly. A spray of glittering mica exploded into the air and sparkled momentarily around the man who wielded the tool as if it were a weapon. Sweat ran in rivulets down Reno Manchahi's drawn, intense face. Naked from the waist up, the hot July sun beating down on his back, he hefted the sledgehammer skyward once more. Muscles in his thick forearms leaped and biceps bulged. Even his breath was focused on the boulder. In his mind's eye, he pictured Army General Robert Hampton's fleshy, arrogant fifty-year-old features on the rock's surface. Air exploded from between his lips as he brought the avenging hammer down. The boulder pulverized beneath his funneled hatred.

One shot...one kill...

Nostrils flaring, he inhaled the dank, humid heat and drew it deep into his massive lungs. Revenge allowed Reno to endure his imprisonment at a U.S. Navy brig near San Diego, California. Drops of sweat were flung in all directions as the crack of his sledge-hammer claimed a third stone victim. Mouth taut, Reno moved to the next boulder.

The other prisoners in the stone yard gave him a wide berth. They always did. They instinctively felt his simmering hatred, the palpable revenge in his cinna-mon-colored eyes, was more than skin-deep.

And they whispered he was different.

Reno enjoyed being a loner for good reason. He came from a medicine family of shape-shifters. But even this secret power had not protected him—or his family. His wife, Ilona, and his three-year-old daughter, Sarah, were dead. Murdered by Army General Hampton in their former home on USMC base in Camp Pendleton, California. Bitterness thrummed through Reno as he savagely pushed the toe of his scarred leather boot against several smaller pieces of gray granite that were in his way.

The sun beat down upon Manchahi's naked shoul-ders, grown dark red over time, shouting his half-Apache heritage. With his straight black hair grazing

LINDSAY McKENNA249

his thick shoulders, copper skin and broad face with high cheekbones, everyone knew he was Indian. When he'd first arrived at the brig, some of the prisoners taunted him and called him Geronimo. Something strange happened to Reno during his fight with the name-calling prisoners. Leaning down after he'd won the scuffle, he'd snarled into each of their bloodied faces that if they were going to call him anything, they would call him *gan,* which was the Apache word for *devil.*

His attackers had been shocked by the wounds on their faces, the deep claw marks. Reno recalled doubling his fist as they'd attacked him en masse. In that split second, he'd gone into an altered state of consciousness. In times of danger, he transformed into a jaguar. A deep, growling sound had emitted from his throat as he defended himself in the three-against-one fracas. It all happened so fast that he thought he had imagined it. He'd seen his hands morph into a forearm and paw, claws extended. The slashes left on the three men's faces after the fight told him he'd begun to shape-shift. A fist made bruises and swelling; not four perfect, deep claw marks. Stunned and anxious, he hid the knowledge of what else he was from these prisoners. Reno's only defense was to make all the prisoners so damned scared of him and remain a loner.

Alone. Yeah, he was alone, all right. The steel hammer swept downward with hellish ferocity. As the granite groaned in protest, Reno shut his eyes for just a moment. Sweat dripped off his nose and square chin.

Straightening, he wiped his furrowed, wet brow and looked into the pale blue sky. What got his attention was the startling cry of a red-tailed hawk as it flew over the brig yard. Squinting, he watched the bird. Reno could make out the rust-colored tail on the hawk. As a kid growing up on the Apache reservation in Arizona, Reno knew that all animals that appeared before him were messengers.

Brother, what message do you bring me? Reno knew one had to ask in order to receive. Allowing the sledgehammer to drop to his side, he concentrated on the hawk who wheeled in tightening circles above him.

Freedom! the hawk cried in return.

Reno shook his head, his black hair moving against his broad, thickset shoulders. *Freedom? No way, Brother. No way.* Figuring that he was making up the hawk's shrill message, Reno turned away. Back to his rocks. Back to picturing Hampton's smug face.

Freedom!

* * * * *

Look for UNFORGIVEN by Lindsay McKenna,
the spine-tingling launch title from
Silhouette Nocturne™.
Available September 26, wherever books are sold.

Silhouette® Desire®

**Introducing an exciting appearance
by legendary
New York Times bestselling author**

DIANA PALMER

HEARTBREAKER

He's the ultimate bachelor…
but he may have just met
the one woman to change his ways!

Join the drama in the story of a confirmed
bachelor, an amnesiac beauty and their
unexpected passionate romance.

**"Diana Palmer is a mesmerizing storyteller
who captures the essence of what
a romance should be."**—*Affaire de Coeur*

Heartbreaker *is available from Silhouette Desire
in September 2006.*

Silhouette® Desire

THE PART-TIME WIFE

by *USA TODAY* bestselling author

Maureen Child

Abby Talbot was the belle of Eastwick society;
the perfect hostess and wife. If only her
husband were more attentiive. But when
she sets out to teach him a lesson and files
for divorce, Abby quickly learns her husband's
true identity...and exposes them to scandals
and drama galore!

On sale October 2006 from Silhouette Desire!

Available wherever books are sold,
including most bookstores, supermarkets,
discount stores and drug stores.

If you enjoyed what you just read,
then we've got an offer you can't resist!

Take 2 bestselling love stories FREE!

Plus get a FREE surprise gift!

Clip this page and mail it to Silhouette Reader Service™

IN U.S.A.
3010 Walden Ave.
P.O. Box 1867
Buffalo, N.Y. 14240-1867

IN CANADA
P.O. Box 609
Fort Erie, Ontario
L2A 5X3

YES! Please send me 2 free Silhouette Special Edition® novels and my free surprise gift. After receiving them, if I don't wish to receive anymore, I can return the shipping statement marked cancel. If I don't cancel, I will receive 6 brand-new novels every month, before they're available in stores! In the U.S.A., bill me at the bargain price of $4.24 plus 25¢ shipping and handling per book and applicable sales tax, if any*. In Canada, bill me at the bargain price of $4.99 plus 25¢ shipping and handling per book and applicable taxes**. That's the complete price and a savings of at least 10% off the cover prices—what a great deal! I understand that accepting the 2 free books and gift places me under no obligation ever to buy any books. I can always return a shipment and cancel at any time. Even if I never buy another book from Silhouette, the 2 free books and gift are mine to keep forever.

235 SDN DZ9D
335 SDN DZ9E

Name	(PLEASE PRINT)	
Address	Apt.#	
City	State/Prov.	Zip/Postal Code

Not valid to current Silhouette Special Edition® subscribers.

Want to try two free books from another series?
Call 1-800-873-8635 or visit www.morefreebooks.com.

* Terms and prices subject to change without notice. Sales tax applicable in N.Y.
** Canadian residents will be charged applicable provincial taxes and GST.
All orders subject to approval. Offer limited to one per household.
® are registered trademarks owned and used by the trademark owner and or its licensee.

SPED04R   ©2004 Harlequin Enterprises Limited

SILHOUETTE

SPECIAL EDITION™

Experience the "magic" of falling in love at Halloween with a new *Holiday Hearts* story!

UNDER HIS SPELL

by KRISTIN HARDY

October 2006

Bad-boy ski racer J. J. Cooper can get any woman he wants—except Lainie Trask. Lainie's grown up with him and vows that nothing he says or does will change her mind. But J.J.'s got his eye on Lainie, and when he moves into her neighborhood and into her life, she finds herself falling under his spell....

HOLIDAY HEARTS

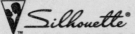

COMING NEXT MONTH

SPECIAL EDITION

#1783 IT TAKES A FAMILY—Victoria Pade
Northbridge Nuptials
Penniless and raising an infant niece after her sister's death, Karis Pratt's only hope was to go to Northbridge, Montana, and find the baby's father, Luke Walker. Did this small-town cop hold the key to renewed family ties and a bright new future for Karis?

#1784 ROCK-A-BYE RANCHER—Judy Duarte
When rugged Clay Callaghan asked attorney Dani De La Cruz to help bring his orphaned granddaughter back from Mexico, Dani couldn't say no to the case...but what would she say to the smitten cattleman's more personal proposals?

#1785 MOTHER IN TRAINING—Marie Ferrarella
Talk of the Neighborhood
When Zooey Finnegan walked out on her fiancé, the gossips pounced. Unfazed, she went on to work wonders as nanny to widower Jack Lever's two kids. But when she got Jack to come out of his own emotional shell...the town *really* had something to talk about!

#1786 UNDER HIS SPELL—Kristin Hardy
Holiday Hearts
Lainie Trask's longtime crush on J. J. Cooper hadn't amounted to much—J.J. seemed too busy with World Cup skiing and womanizing to notice the feisty curator. But an injury led to big changes for J.J.—including plenty of downtime to discover Lainie's charms....

#1787 LOVE LESSONS—Gina Wilkins
Medical researcher Dr. Catherine Travis had all the trappings of the good life...except for someone special to share it with. Would maintenance man and part-time college student Mike Clancy fix what ailed the good doctor...despite the odds arrayed against them?

#1788 NOT YOUR AVERAGE COWBOY—
Christine Wenger
When rancher Buck Porter invited famous cookbook author and city slicker Merry Turner to help give Rattlesnake Ranch a makeover, it was a recipe for trouble. So what was the secret ingredient that soon made the cowboy, his young daughter and Merry inseparable?

SSECNM0906